'You haven'...
you?'

Warm brown eyes peered at him across the top of the towel.

'Why on earth would I be crying? I've been running around with paint on my face all day so I thought I'd wash it off.'

Jacinta was pleased the excuse sounded so reasonable. She could hardly have told him splashing her face with cold water had been an attempt to cure the tingles he caused.

But first his voice, then the sight of him, had brought them back a thousandfold.

She was battling the renewed attack when she saw the blood on the snowy white handkerchief he held in his hand. She crossed the room and took his hand in hers.

She looked up at him and saw something in the grey-green of his eyes that stopped both the tingles and her breath. She couldn't bring herself to release his hand—and her brain had stopped working.

Also her lungs.

And possibly her heart.

Previously a teacher, shopkeeper, travel agent, pig farmer, builder and worker in the disability field (among other things), the 'writing bug' struck **Meredith Webber** unexpectedly. She entered a competition run by a women's magazine, shared the third prize with two hundred and fifty other would-be writers, and found herself infected. Thirty-something books later, she's still suffering. She says, 'Medical romances appeal to me because they offer the opportunity to include a wider cast of characters, and the challenge of interweaving a love story into the drama of medical or paramedical practice.'

Recent titles by the same author:

HER DR WRIGHT
A WOMAN WORTH WAITING FOR
THE TEMPTATION TEST
A VERY PRECIOUS GIFT

THE MARRIAGE GAMBLE

BY
MEREDITH WEBBER

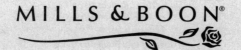

MILLS & BOON

All the characters in this book have no existence outside the imagination of the author, and have no relation whatsoever to anyone bearing the same name or names. They are not even distantly inspired by any individual known or unknown to the author, and all the incidents are pure invention.

*First published in Great Britain 2002
Harlequin Mills & Boon Limited,
Eton House, 18-24 Paradise Road, Richmond, Surrey TW9 1SR*

© Meredith Webber 2002

ISBN 0 263 83077 2

*Set in Times Roman 10 on 11 pt.
03-0702-56076*

*Printed and bound in Spain
by Litografía Rosés, S.A., Barcelona*

CHAPTER ONE

MICHAEL TRENT stood in front of the painting, which three eminent artists and critics had adjudged the best in the exhibition, and frowned. He hadn't yet seen the bill for the air fares and accommodation for these same judges, but he guessed it would be hefty, though not as hefty as the acquisition prize of twenty thousand dollars Trent Medical Clinics, as sponsors of the art award, had offered.

'A cross-section of a wart, with a phloxine-tartrazine stain, seen through a pathologist's electron microscope.'

He was startled by the voice at his elbow, but amused enough by the description to smile.

'I'll admit to not spending a lot of time studying cross-sections of warts,' he said to the diminutive brunette who'd materialised beside him to offer her opinion of the striated lines of colour, broken by spotty blobs of darker paint, 'but I *had* been thinking about slides and smears and images from my early student days.'

He paused, unconsciously assimilating twin arcs of dark eyebrows, eyes so brown they were almost black, a neat nose and sweetly curving lips—glossed but not coloured—before he added, 'Is it as bad as I think it is?'

His fellow viewer tipped her head to one side as if to better consider the painting. She had dark hair, pulled loosely back and held with a clasp, and the movement brought an attractive sheen to it.

'I suppose the actual composition isn't too bad—I mean, it's got a kind of balanced look with those amoeba-like things on one side and the striated muscle fibres on the other. And the main colour combinations of pink and purple, while not what I'd choose for home decorating, aren't as gloomy as the all black and grey masterpiece that won the highly commended award. It looks like diseased lung tissue.'

Her opinion of the highly commended so matched his own that he was about to introduce himself and ask her which of the exhibits she *did* like when Jaclyn tapped his shoulder.

'Darling, you simply must meet Beau Delpratt. He's so delighted with the win he's offered to do a complementary painting to hang opposite this one.'

'Complimentary as in free?' Michael asked, and Jaclyn gave a trill of laughter.

'Oh, darling, as if you could expect Delpratt to *give* his talent away.'

Jaclyn's hand slipped to his forearm and she applied a slight pressure which, while unspoken, definitely meant, Come with me now.

Prepared to follow—after all, he'd known talking to the artist would be part of his duties for the evening—he was momentarily distracted by the word 'Talent?' murmured in a huskily mocking voice behind him.

He turned back but the brunette was still studying the painting, so motionless he thought he must have imagined hearing the word. As he threaded his way through the crowd of expensively dressed men and women, responding to greetings and praise with a nod or murmured 'thank you', he wondered who she was and whether, in a crush like this, he might happen to meet up with her again.

'Great start!' Jacinta muttered to herself. Coming to the art show opening had seemed such a good way to meet the big boss, Michael Trent. Then she'd seen the painting to which he was giving the major prize and had blurted out the first thing that had come into her head.

Or maybe it had been the shock of seeing the man himself. In the flesh. For the first time.

Hunky men had been so thin on the ground in her vicinity in recent years she'd begun to think they only existed between the covers of expensive magazines.

To be honest, healthy men of any type had been thin on the

ground, which probably explained the tingly feeling his voice had generated in her stomach. She'd always been a sucker for deep gravelly voices.

So she'd shot off her mouth about the prize-winning painting!

Though he hadn't seemed put out by her remark, rather the opposite, in fact, which had encouraged her to make an even more derogatory remark about the second place-getter.

Then the willowy blonde had appeared and effortlessly removed him from in front of the painting, and Jacinta was left staring blankly at the pink and purple swirls, which failed to provide any inspiration for her next move.

Following him through the crowd and appearing at his side a second time wouldn't offer the element of surprise she'd hoped might lead to a conversation that ranged beyond the artwork on the walls. But trying to get an appointment with him at his office hadn't worked and neither had phoning him at home. The man was surrounded by more minders than Michael Jackson!

No! It had to be tonight. Somehow she had to get close to him again.

'Drink, madam?'

A waiter pressed a tray towards her, using his free hand to indicate the different drinks on offer.

'Champagne, dry white wine, Chardonnay.'

'Not right now,' Jacinta told him, as the germ of an idea sprouted in her mind.

The drink waiters wore black trousers and charcoal grey shirts—no doubt to differentiate them from the dinner-suited male guests. But the women serving finger food were in black—long skirts, and roll-neck, long-sleeved, skivvy tops. Not so different to Jacinta's dress with its high neck and long sleeves.

She made her purposefully towards the kitchen area, where the caterers were refilling platters to pass around again. Given his opinion of Beau Delpratt's winning entry, Michael Trent might welcome a diversion. And as he chose between dainty little omelette rolls filled with sour cream and smoked salmon or herbed pikelets topped with horseradish cream and tiny prawns, she could introduce herself and tell him she had to speak to him about Abbott Road. Quickly explain she'd been unable to get an appointment any other way.

Should be a cinch!

So, why, as she made her way towards him, was her stomach churning like a washing machine?

No, washing machines sloshed while her stomach's behaviour was more a grumble of uneasiness. What else might churn?

Seeking a suitable metaphor took her closer to where Michael Trent's height made him easily identifiable, but the knot of people around him added to the anxiety that had replaced the tingle in Jacinta's midsection.

'Ah, more food,' someone on the outskirts of the knot cried, and half a dozen hands reached out to scoop the small delicacies off the plate.

'There's plenty coming,' Jacinta assured them, while inwardly fuming at the gluttony which was rapidly diminishing her excuse to get close to Dr Trent. 'These were for the officials,' she tried, wanting to slap their hands away, but one man was passing pikelets to all his friends, and before the words were out, all she had left on the platter were a few sprigs of parsley and a tired lettuce leaf.

'It's a wonder they didn't eat those as well,' she muttered to herself as she pushed her way back to the kitchen to refill the tray and start again. 'And the platter, the pigs!'

'What's this, Jazzy? You moonlighting as a waitress? Surely those days are over for you.'

Adam Lockyer accosted her before she was halfway back to her destination.

'Ah, but you're working for Mike now, I hear. Is this his way of making staff feel part of the empire? Expecting them to help out at functions?'

Adam was smiling jovially down at her, while his blue eyes

flicked an admiring glance up and down her person. He really was the world's worst flirt!

Her mind was trying to devise a new strategy so she wasn't paying a hundred per cent attention to Adam's light-hearted prattle, but the name Mike was recurring with regularity and finally registered in her frustrated brain.

'Mike? You call Michael Trent Mike? You know him?'

Adam looked a little put out, no doubt by Jacinta's incredulity.

'Why shouldn't I know him? We're both doctors after all. In fact, we trained together, down in Sydney. Knew him from playing rugby before that. He was a state player and could have gone on to play for Australia. Don't know why he dropped out.'

Jacinta could have told him. She'd studied every bit of information she could find on Michael Trent, but she guessed Adam wasn't particularly interested in knowing anyway, and right now he could be put to better use.

'I'll just return this tray, then you can introduce me to him,' she told Adam, taking hold of his arm so he couldn't escape her. 'Make it casual. Let him think we're together, and you're greeting him as an old friend and introducing the woman you're with.'

Adam gazed down at her with such perplexity she suspected the task would be beyond him. How the man had ever made it through medical school…

'It's not hard,' she assured him, then a sudden doubt assailed her. 'You haven't already said hello to him, have you? Or introduced him to your date?'

'I don't have a date,' Adam said, beaming now she'd asked him something simple enough for him to answer. 'I always come to these things alone. Never fail to meet someone who wants to go on afterwards.'

He smiled hopefully at her.

'I don't suppose you'd—'

Jacinta shook her head.

'We tried it years ago, Adam,' she reminded him. 'After

Becky and Paul's wedding. One date, and we both realised we were only ever going to be friends.'

'Most women would have been thrilled to spend the day in the champagne tent at a big race meeting,' he grumbled, while Jacinta deposited the tray on the serving bench, then took her friend by the arm and steered him back towards their destination.

'I'm not most women,' she reminded him. 'Now, have you got it right? We breeze up to him, you do the "old mate" thing and introduce me. Then, if you wouldn't mind distracting anyone who's hanging around him—you could tell that story about the Irish basketballer—I can have a quick word with Michael.'

'But you work for him—you could have a quick word anytime.'

Jacinta sighed. Of all the allies she could have chosen, she'd been stuck with Adam, to whom the world was black and white and whose interests—outside paediatrics, at which he was very good—were limited to women, racehorses and sporting stars.

'I work in the Abbott Road clinic which is light years away from the rarefied air of his Forest Glen home. And he's so hemmed in by staff it's impossible to get a memo through to him.'

Or if he does get it, he ignores it, she added darkly, but only in her head.

'So you want to talk to him about something?' Adam said, far too loudly given they'd now reached the outskirts of the crowd around one of the city's wealthiest men.

Uttering a silent prayer for patience, Jacinta smiled and nodded, then, as Adam's broad shoulders forced a wedge through the cluster, she clutched at the bottom of his jacket and followed in his wake.

'Mike, old man! Long time no see!'

I could have taken a bet he'd say that, Jacinta thought, but Adam had got her to where she wanted to be so she could hardly criticise his conversational gambits.

'How's everything going? I heard you'd opened another clinic. That's five or six, is it?'

Michael Trent greeted Adam with a smile and hearty handshake, asked how the ankle-biter business was going and generally seemed pleased to see his old rugby friend.

'Oh, almost forgot!' Adam said, when he and Michael had relived several ancient games and played 'do you remember' about their university lecturers. 'Got someone I want you to meet. Very special little woman, this one.'

He hauled Jacinta forward before she had time to kick him, hard, in the shins. Little woman indeed!

'Jacinta Ford. Michael Trent.'

'Ah, the wart!' Michael Trent said, holding out his hand towards Jacinta. 'Jacinta—that's a pretty name.'

'But too much of a mouthful,' Adam put in. 'Just call her Jazzy!'

Jacinta, who'd spent three months of her hospital training working under Adam and trying to convince him she hated her childhood nickname, sent Michael Trent a look that dared him to try it.

'I prefer Jacinta,' she said in her coolest voice, then remembered her ulterior motive in meeting the man and smiled to make up for the coolness.

Mike accepted the small hand she offered and murmured a polite greeting, while random thoughts flashed through his head. How delicate, almost fragile, her hand felt in his much larger one, how her smile lit up her face, how strange he'd met up with her again without having to go seek her.

Ah, but she was with Adam Lockyer, the man voted most likely to succeed—with women—way back when they'd gone through medical school together.

The killjoy in him squelched the pleasure.

He was consoling himself with the thought that personally he preferred blondes to brunettes, and that small women always made him feel overly large and clumsy, when he realised she was talking to him.

Urgently.

'So, you see, if I could just set up a time to talk to you,' she was saying, when Jaclyn, with perfect timing, once again grasped his arm. 'I know we could work something out.'

Brown eyes, luminously large in her small face, gazed beguilingly up into his, while a quite becoming flush lit the clear skin.

'Darling, they're ready for the presentation,' Jaclyn was saying in his ear, while her hand was exerting a similar pressure on his arm. 'We really must go.'

She smiled apologetically at Adam—women always smiled at Adam—but ignored his companion, and it was partly out of embarrassment at Jaclyn's behaviour that Mike gave in.

'No problem,' he assured Jacinta-not-Jazzy. 'Phone my secretary and set it up.'

He turned to follow his arm, which Jaclyn was tugging through the crowd, but his way was blocked by the small woman who'd stepped abruptly into his path. The beguiling brown eyes were now shooting sparks of anger and the becoming flush in her cheeks had turned to red flags of rage.

'I have phoned your secretary seventeen times, I have spoken to every underling and yes-man in your employ. I have sent you written memos, emails and faxes, all requesting an appointment and all answered by faceless minions who assure me you understand my concerns and are taking them into consideration.'

She stamped her foot at that stage, but missed the floor and got his toe—the one with the ingrown toenail he kept meaning to have fixed.

'Shit!'

The word reverberated through the room, causing beautifully clad women and elegantly suited men to turn towards him. Not that he cared. He was hopping up and down, clutching at his foot, wanting only to take off his shoe and sit for a while until the agony subsided.

The cause of his problems, meanwhile, gave him a stricken look then, perhaps realising his pain went beyond a simple toe-stamp, dropped down, wresting his injured foot from his hands and balancing it on her knee while she carefully undid the laces of his shoes.

'Leave it alone!' He managed to put enough menace into the whispered order for her to stop, which was just as well because if she'd removed the shoe and hurt the toe in doing it, he'd probably have strangled her.

She looked up enquiringly at him, her fingers still hovering over the laces.

Pretending a calmness he was far from feeling, he added, with less menace but sufficient warning to make his message clear, 'It's only throbbing. It'll get better soon. If you take the shoe off, it will hurt more putting it back on.'

She stopped trying to remove the shoe but retained her grasp on his foot, moving it enough to disturb his precarious balance.

'Just name a time,' she said, and as most of the crowd had either moved off towards the centre of the gallery for the presentation or had shifted away from him in case he crashed down on them, only he heard the veiled threat in her low-pitched voice or saw the determination in the dark eyes.

If she lifted his foot he *would* crash to the ground, but if she pressed on his toe...

'Tonight.' Fear of more pain lent desperation to his voice. 'I won't be needed once the prizes are handed out. I'll ask Don Jacobs, the gallery owner, if we can use his office. It's towards the back, you can't miss it.' He glanced at his watch, worked out how long it would take to get from the gallery to the Hilton where he was due to deliver an after-dinner speech at ten then added, 'I can give you ten minutes. Just wait by the door.'

She looked so angry he thought for a moment she was going to lift his foot and tip him off balance anyway, but in the end she let go, satisfying herself with a final glare in his direction.

Ten minutes is better than nothing, Jacinta told herself. In ten minutes, surely you can convince him to come down to Abbott Road and see conditions for himself. After all, he must have some feeling for the place—it was where he started out, the foundation of his empire.

She thanked Adam for helping her to her feet, thanked him again for the introduction, then reminded him the official presentation would signal the beginning of the end of the art show opening and he'd better start circulating if he wanted to find someone who'd go on to dinner or a nightclub with him after it.

'But I thought you might change your mind,' he protested. 'It's an age since we caught up with each other.'

Jacinta smiled at him.

'We can do that in ten seconds. I'm still working with people from low socio-economic backgrounds and you're still overcharging wealthy anxious parents who want to be sure they have the healthiest and most intelligent children in the universe.'

'I also do public hospital rounds,' he reminded her, sounding so aggrieved she reached up to kiss him on the cheek.

'I know you do, and all your patients, as well as all their parents, love you dearly. Now, go and find yourself a nice woman to take out to dinner.'

She turned him around and pushed him gently in the direction of the bulk of the gathering, then made her way towards the back of the long gallery, where she found a small, glassed-in office.

After a month of frustration, she'd finally made contact with Michael Trent.

So why didn't she feel more satisfaction?

Because he was six feet tall, far too handsome for his own good and his voice had made her stomach tingle.

This is business, she reminded herself when her mind showed interest in following up the tingling phenomenon.

Business!

Though her toes were curling a bit as well. Could the champagne be responsible? She'd had a quick glass for Dutch courage before approaching him by the painting.

She shifted from one foot to the other and peered through the glass into the gallery owner's office. A small but exquisite painting, a seaside scene with sun shining on blue water, hung

on the wall behind the gallery owner's desk, and Jacinta, grate-
fully distracted by its beauty, was studying it when a voice—
the voice—accosted her.

'So, Jacinta Ford, come on in and tell me why you've been
so desperate to get in touch with me.'

Michael Trent unlocked the door, then stood back to let her
enter the office first. Walking past him made her feel even
shorter than usual, and she wondered if he'd done it deliberately.

The thought stiffened her determination, though the sharp
tang of aftershave she'd caught as she'd passed him lingered
in some olfactory memory box, taunting her efforts.

He walked—well, limped—past her and, as if by right,
dropped into the chair behind the desk. Now he latched his
hands behind his head and stretched back, tilting the chair so
it balanced on the two back legs. The ultimate corporate mo-
gul!

'I should tell you from the outset that my charity dollars are
committed for the year, I'll only do one art prize and that's in
conjunction with this gallery and, no, I have no need of an
advertising agency, a publicist, a fashion guru or an image
consultant.'

She had no doubt he was trying to intimidate her but she
was more confused than intimidated, and no matter how often
she repeated his statement in her head, she still couldn't make
sense of it. Hopefully, she didn't look as bemused as she felt.

'Why would you imagine I thought you needed an image
consultant?' she managed, latching onto the last of his job
descriptions while studying the image in question. His dinner
suit had obviously been made for him, fitting his tall, broad-
shouldered figure to perfection, and with his black, silver-
flecked hair, craggy features and arresting eyes, he was already
a photographer's dream.

Especially a female photographer…

'An image consultant?' She repeated the words, shaking her
head in disbelief.

He shrugged off her astonishment.

'People representing such agencies have all, at some time or another, used elaborate ploys to gain an interview with me. I feel it's only fair to warn them at the outset that I'm not interested.' He checked his watch. 'You've seven minutes left.'

'Seven minutes is more than enough,' she snapped, infuriated by his disdainful attitude. Not to mention the conceit of the man! 'In fact, seven seconds would probably do to get the main point across. Your clinic at Abbott Road is a disgrace. It's dank and dirty and dreary and probably makes patients unfortunate enough to end up there even sicker and more depressed than they were when they came in. Now, I'm perfectly willing to do what I can to improve the place, but I need your permission. Yes or no?'

She was a little virago! He'd once looked up the meaning of the word after reading a book published by the Virago company. This turbulent, scolding woman seemed to fit the description admirably. But finding a word that fitted her didn't help him understand what she was going on about. Abbott Road being a disgrace?

'In what way?' he asked, conscious of the fact he'd have to leave very shortly.

'Well, paint, for one thing,' she replied, which threw him into even worse confusion.

'Paint? I run a medical clinic, not art classes.'

'The paint on the walls!'

Ah!

'The paint's peeling? Is that the problem?'

'Didn't you listen to anything I said?' she raged, and Mike suspected if she'd been two feet taller and a man she'd have socked him on the jaw. 'The whole place is a disgrace. Come down from your ivory tower and check it out some time. See what your "business manager" thinks is suitable for Abbott Road. Take a look at the place, sit in the waiting room, flick through a grime-encrusted magazine. That is, of course, if your busy social life allows you an hour now and then to venture into the real world.'

She must be a patient down there, Mike realised. No wonder she hadn't been able to get in touch with him. Patients saw the practising doctors at all his clinics—or spoke to his secretaries. It must be what, three years, since he'd done any hands-on doctoring, and then it had only been a week to fulfil an obligation to a friend. But she didn't need to know that, and appeasing her should be easy. After all, as a patient the most she'd be there was for fifteen minutes at a time. He could send Barry, his business manager, or maybe Christine, Barry's assistant, to check the place out and she'd never know he hadn't been in person.

'I hadn't realised things were so bad,' he said in his best conciliatory tone. 'I'll get down there this week.'

'Good,' the woman said, and he was congratulating himself on getting out of the situation so lightly when she added, 'And make sure you have more than seven minutes. An hour would barely scratch the surface.'

Mike collected Jaclyn and drove to the Hilton, delivered his speech to two hundred selected guests, mingled for an hour to be polite then dropped Jaclyn at her luxury unit in the city, refusing her invitation to stay by pleading tiredness.

But as he drove along the river towards his home in an upmarket riverside suburb, he remembered the brunette's face, not so much the neat features, dark eyes, soft lips and the perfect arches of her eyebrows, but the fire and passion that had lit it from within.

Bloody exhausting all that fire and passion, he reminded himself. Thank heavens as we get older common sense and sound business principles supersede it.

But the mention of Abbott Road had brought back memories of when he'd had the fire and passion—when he'd thrown all his energies into setting up that first inner-city medical clinic.

He turned away from the river, feeling the engine shift to a lower gear as he drove up the steep hill towards his house. High on an escarpment overlooking the river, and beyond it the city lights, it was not only in a prime position but was one of a handful of heritage-listed houses in the area—the ultimate status symbol.

But tonight his feeling of satisfaction in his hard-won achievements was lacking, and the light on in the library of his house suggested things weren't going to get any better.

'That you, Mike?'

His father had greeted him the same way all his life, and Mike was often tempted to ask whom he thought it might be.

'You're up late, Dad,' he said, crossing the hall and entering the library, then bending to drop a kiss on his father's greying hair. In just this way, his father, so manly a man, had kissed him goodbye every day of his childhood. Who was it had said the child was father of the man?

'I keep having to take sidetracks with these old Greek chaps,' Ted Trent told him. 'I'm reading Aristotle and he mentions Socrates and I have to find that fellow to see what he has to say for himself.'

He waved his hands towards the wall of bookshelves where a small fork-lift had been adapted so he could roll his wheelchair onto a platform and raise himself up to find a particular book, or range along the shelves in search of it.

'Very time-consuming,' Mike agreed, marvelling, as he always did, that this working-class man who'd had little education could read and understand the writings of the world's great philosophers.

And get such pleasure from his pursuit of knowledge and understanding!

'Libby phoned to say she won't be coming tomorrow. Something on at school. She had her usual grumble about the teachers but sounded really bright.'

Disappointment warred with relief. He loved his daughter dearly, but at twelve the simple pleasures they'd once shared—going on picnics in the mountains, a day at the beach—had become 'so boring, Dad' that he'd begun to dread her visits as much as he anticipated them. Especially since she'd started bringing a clutch of friends with her, and the

house had seemed overrun by very skimpily clad young fe-
males.

'Well, now we won't have a houseful of twelve-year-olds
giggling around the place, do you want to do something special? We could take the boat down the bay.'

'Sorry, son! Jack and I are off to the Darling Downs. It's
one of those old codgers' trips and we heard a couple of new
widows are going along. The bus'll pick us up at seven. I'd
left you a note as I didn't think I'd see you.'

Which means he thought I'd spend the night with Jaclyn.
Mike was irritated by the assumption. He hadn't yet reached
that stage of a relationship with her and, though he was
tempted and knew she was willing, he was finding himself
more and more reluctant to get too involved.

Having a twelve-year-old daughter was part of it. In the
past, Libby had accepted any woman who'd happened to come
on picnics with them as Dad's friend. But there'd been a very
knowing glint in her eye when she'd first met Jaclyn a couple
of weeks ago. Knowing enough to make Mike draw back from
committing himself any further.

For the moment!

'Now, seeing you *are* here, tell me about the show.'

Mike settled into one of the comfortable leather armchairs,
propped the foot with the still aching toe on a footstool and
resigned himself to the task. His father might have a better
social life than he did these days, but it didn't stop the old
man wanting to know all the details of Mike's day—a habit
that had started when Mike had been a kid at school. Then
he'd sat at the kitchen table, watching his father cook their
evening meal, and had enjoyed sharing the small disappoint-
ments or triumphs of the day.

At thirty-eight, there were nights when he'd rather have
gone straight to bed!

Mike woke in the morning, after an unsettled night's sleep, to
an empty house and the prospect of a full day where he'd set
aside all work plans and now had nothing to do.

He rolled over in bed and lifted the phone. The unsettled night had got him thinking about his relationship with Jaclyn. Maybe it was time to take it further. He'd phone her, see if she'd like to join him for breakfast at one of the riverside restaurants. Who knew what would follow?

Then a glance at the clock told him that ten past seven was too early to be phoning anyone. It must have been the bus departing with his father and Jack that had woken him. He'd go back to sleep.

At seven-thirty, frustrated by being unable to sleep late when given the chance, he climbed out of bed, winced as his sore toe hit the floor, showered, dressed in 'round the house' type clothes, then made himself a cup of coffee while he considered what to do.

All day.

He needed some exercise but his toe was still throbbing, so that was out.

There was always work. He could go to the office. The medical web-site he'd been setting up had taken all of his time lately, but Sid Chase had brought in the architectural drawings for the new clinic and he had to look at them some time. And Paul, his accountant, was a workaholic. He'd phone him up, suggest a working lunch to discuss financing the project. Paul was all for him divesting some of his less viable properties rather than borrowing for this.

Abbott Road!

He remembered the dark-haired woman and smiled to himself. 'Give yourself more than an hour!' she'd told him, with enough scorn to shrivel a lesser man.

Well, he had more than hour. He had an entire day. He'd go back to where it all began—take a look at Abbott Road.

CHAPTER TWO

EASIER said than done. He could get to Abbott Road, no problem, but how to get in to the clinic? He could phone the clinic's office manager—which would arouse immediate suspicion in that woman's breast. She'd assume she was in trouble—people always did—and insist on accompanying him, which would spoil what he was beginning to think of as a sentimental journey.

Who else would have keys? No doubt the medical staff, but he didn't know any of them personally. Chris Welsh, who'd started with him at Abbott Road, now appointed all the doctors, and Jill Claybourne, who'd been their nurse-receptionist in those early days, was in charge of the nursing staff.

Calling either of them would raise more questions than he wished to answer. Both knew he was thinking of selling the place, and both had argued against it—though they'd both done well out of Trent Clinics and should understand by now there was no place for sentiment in business decisions.

Security people must have keys. They were on call twenty-four hours a day to answer the alarms. Mike had to check the discreet sign on the outside of the kitchen window to recall the name of the firm who did all his security, then, once connected, go through the third-degree, trying to prove he was who he said he was.

'Look,' he said, when the argument had raised his temper to near-explosion point, 'get your boss, or whoever has authority to hand over keys, down to your office. I'll be there in fifteen minutes with enough ID to satisfy a police investigation, and I'll want to collect that key, or I'll tear up the contract I have with your firm.'

He got the key, but the victory brought him little joy. The

21

head of the security firm had asked if Karen had had her baby yet, and Mike, unwilling to admit he knew no Karen, pregnant or otherwise, had mumbled something he'd hoped was non-committal and changed the subject. It had simply been a reminder of how out of touch he'd become.

School was more interesting for his daughter than spending a day with her dad, he didn't know the names of his employees and firms whose existence depended on their contracts with him had never realised he existed, content to do business with whoever headed their particular branch of his organisation.

He drove to the city, parked his car and walked down the pedestrian mall in the centre of the city. When he'd first opened the clinic, it had been a busy thoroughfare, but it was now blocked off to all but emergency vehicles. Trees and shade-cloth sails provided shelter, while seats offered resting places for weary feet. Being Sunday, it was near deserted, the tables and chairs from the sidewalk cafés stacked away.

There was the old pharmacy where Lauren had worked when he'd first met her. She'd been as excited as he had over the clinic in the beginning—or had she always seen it as a means to an end?

The pharmacy had been renovated, with pinkish coloured tiles covering the old brick façade, making it look modern and inviting.

Making the doorway to the clinic seem dim and dark in comparison.

He moved on and stood in front of the small entrance where steps led down to the basement he'd turned into an inner-city clinic thirteen years ago. Of course, as the clinic was closed, most of the lights were off. That would explain why it looked so dark and uninviting. The dim light above the stairs was probably a safety precaution.

Mike walked past the entrance and frowned. He'd eventually bought the building that housed the clinic but surely there'd always been a snack bar in the ground floor shop. When had it closed? And who'd approved the lease to what called itself an adult bookshop, but from the window display sold far more than books? Right next to a medical clinic children could be attending!

For the second time that morning, a sense that he'd lost control of his business threatened to overwhelm him and for a fraction of a second, fearing more self-revelation might be in store, he considered ignoring the clinic altogether. But he'd said he'd visit and visit he would. He'd also find out who'd approved the lease of the ground-floor shop—he made a mental note of it—so it couldn't happen in any other premises he owned.

Having made his way cautiously down the steps, aware that the slightest mis-step might send him crashing to the bottom, he was inserting the key into the lock when he heard voices.

Medical clinics had long been targets for drug addicts and why would desperate people take any notice of a small sign stating no drugs or money were kept on the premises?

All senses on full alert, he turned the key in the lock. In his mind, he pictured the place. The door led straight into a waiting room, made narrow by the reception area and treatment room he'd built against the right-hand wall. At the end of the room, three doors opened into three consulting rooms, while a fourth door, in the left-hand wall, opened into a passage that led to washrooms and eventually, because the land sloped away, gave access to a paved area out the back with parking for cars and a separate area for the collection of dustbins.

Whoever was in there must have come that way, for there was no sign of this lock being forced or the hinges jimmied.

Mike inched the door open, remembering the security company's instructions. Back and front doors were alarmed separately, so when you opened the front door you had to neutralise the alarm within thirty seconds of going in, then if you decided to open the back door, you had to disarm that alarm as well.

If he took his time opening the door, the alarm would go off, the intruder would flee, presumably through the back door, the way he'd come in, and Mike wouldn't have to face a crazy with a knife or gun.

When the door had been partially open at least a minute and no alarm had gone off, he made another mental note to speak to someone. The list, starting with 'Who is Karen?' and 'Why an adult bookshop?' was growing.

He could no longer hear voices, but perhaps the music was drowning them out. Wasn't there a requirement for thieves to be as quiet as they could manage—not go around blasting pop music while they robbed and plundered?

With the music making extreme caution less urgent, he pushed the door fully open, though he'd seen enough cop shows on television to keep back against the passage wall in case whoever was in there had a gun.

Not a gun, but a paint-roller.

Peeling himself from the wall, grateful the roller-wielder, a youthful apprentice from the look of him and the amount of spilled paint, had his back to him so hadn't witnessed his cowardice, Mike stepped gingerly into the waiting room.

'Good morning,' he said, glad his heartbeats had returned to somewhere near normal so his voice didn't come out as a feeble mutter. If it had, it wouldn't have been heard above the music issuing from a bright purple radio on the floor behind the painter. 'I'm Michael Trent, the owner of this building. I didn't realise the painting had been scheduled for this week-end.'

The painter let out a squeal—perhaps it was more a scream—at the same time spinning around and flinging the paint-roller in his direction, not connecting but splashing him with bright yellow paint nonetheless.

Not a youthful apprentice at all, but his virago from the previous evening! A knitted cap hid her hair, and that, with the jeans and checked shirt, had made him think the figure had been that of a male.

She'd done a classic double-take when she'd realised who she'd been flinging paint-rollers at, but if he'd thought she was going to apologise for her instinctive reaction, he was mistaken.

She snapped off the radio and headed towards him.

'That bloody alarm didn't go off again. I've told Carmel the darned things are no good. I'm sorry about the paint, but you shouldn't creep up on people and frighten the wits out of them.'

She scrabbled around, retrieving the paint-roller and dabbing an equally paint-soaked rag over the nearby furniture.

'Not that these seats don't look better with a bit of daffodil yellow spotted over them,' she muttered to herself, advancing towards Mike with both the roller and the cloth—no doubt ready to do more damage.

'Put them both down,' he ordered, backing out of the way. 'What kind of paint is it? It's only on my shirt and if it's water-based, I can get it out if I wash it straight away.'

Jacinta retreated, but Michael Trent passed her in two strides, pulling up beside the paint supplies she'd stacked by the wall. Apparently satisfied the paint was indeed water-based, he was now stripping off his shirt.

To reveal a surprisingly well-sculpted upper body.

She stared at it, fascinated by the contours and too terrified by the consequences of hurling a paint-roller at her boss to raise her eyes to his face.

'I assume the washroom's still out this way?' he said, then walked off before she could gasp out a reply—leaving her with a view of an equally impressive back.

You wanted him to come, to take a look at the place, she reminded herself. Then she saw the room through his eyes. She'd started her efforts with the paint-roller on the long left-hand wall and, apart from the fact she hadn't yet got up to do the fiddly edge bit near the ceiling, it looked quite good. But where she'd been working when he'd sneaked in was around the doors leading into the consulting rooms and, because she'd thought she'd finish all the roller bits first, she had broad sweeps of paint above and between the doors, with the remnants of the old dark green colour awaiting the brushwork around the edges.

It looked terrible!

'Did I actually say yes? Or have you jumped the gun?'

He'd crept up on her again and the questions made her start—a sure sign of guilt—but as he was asking, maybe he wouldn't remember.

She'd once read that looking into someone's eyes gave you the appearance of being truthful. She looked into his eyes—a pale colour she couldn't distinguish in the waiting room's appalling lighting, but last night she'd thought them grey—and prepared to lie.

'Don't bother,' he said, as if reading her mind. 'The questions were purely rhetorical. I said I'd call in, not that you could go ahead and paint the place.'

His supercilious tone infuriated Jacinta.

'And why should I have believed you?' she stormed. 'The way you spoke last night, it was more likely you'd have sent an underling, who'd have talked to Carmel, who'd have told whoever it was that the clinic was doing so badly it wasn't worth wasting money on it. Look at it! Do you wonder it's doing badly? People walk in here and imagine they're going to catch something far worse than they've already got just by sitting down in one of the chairs. In fact, most of the patients prefer to stand.'

'And is painting the walls going to reassure them?' He glanced towards the paint-spattered chair. 'Unless you're going to paint the chairs as well.'

For a moment Jacinta regretted putting down the paint-roller. She could have hit him with it. But antagonising the man would make things worse, not better.

'I'm going to replace the chairs,' she said, mustering what dignity she could. 'That was one of the things I wanted to speak to you about.'

'But isn't Carmel right? If the clinic's doing badly, why waste money on it?'

He made the question sound so reasonable that Jacinta forgot the antagonising thing.

'The clinic's doing badly because no one will spend money on it. It's probably one of the most needed services in the inner city, but people are staying away in droves because it's

dank and gloomy and so depressing they must begin to wonder
if it's not a waiting room to hell. Patients don't even have
names, just numbers, and a disembodied voice calls out
"Number twenty-seven to Room Three" and everyone checks
their numbers, and because the numbers aren't given out in
sequence, the person with seventy-five, who might be next,
thinks he's going to be here for three hours so he decides he's
not that sick, drops his number on the floor and sneaks out.'

She glared up at the man she saw as the cause of all these
problems, and was surprised to see not anger but disbelief in
his eyes.

'Patients have numbers?'

Disbelief in his voice as well, but Jacinta wasn't going to
fall for that act.

'Don't tell me you didn't know!' she snorted. 'According
to Carmel, it's the practice now in all your clinics—in the
interests of efficiency, she says, but presumably it's all to do
with money. I suppose it takes less time to call out "number
fourteen" than "Mrs Welby-Sims", though you'd think "Mr
Smith" would be easier to say than "number one hundred and
forty-eight".'

Mike stared at the virago. Not that she was being so virago-
ish now. She was simply yabbering on and making no sense
whatsoever.

'You're saying all the patients are called by number?' He
was aware he was repeating himself but it seemed so unbelievable he had to make sure he had it right before he sacked
someone.

But who? His office manager? Barry, his managerial head?
Himself, for being so immersed in the new projects he'd lost
track of what was happening in the old ones?

'It's supposedly cost-effective,' the woman said, her voice
less forceful now. Maybe some of his disbelief was filtering
through to her.

He slumped down into the nearest chair, realised it was
paint-spattered and unless the paint had dried really quickly

he would now have paint on his trousers. It would just have to stay there. He could hardly take *them* off and wash them.

'Sit down,' he said, waving Jacinta to a cleaner chair. 'For a start, who are you and what business is it of yours whether the place works or not?'

She frowned at him, flopped into a chair, then immediately shot out of it.

'It's not that grubby,' he protested, and she flashed a grin at him.

'It's not the chair, it's the paint. I need to finish what's in the tray or it will get a skin on it and the roller will dry out. Can we talk while I work?'

Mike nodded, still caught up in how the grin had illuminated her face, bringing the neat features alive. But as she pushed the roller through the paint tray then lifted it to the wall he took in the patched appearance of the wall, and the extent of the job she'd undertaken.

'Were you planning on getting all this done today?' he asked, 'or did you feel having it half-done would encourage more customers?'

The look she flashed him this time was totally lacking in amusement.

'I'll get it done today,' she said grimly, and he fancied he heard a silent 'if it kills me' following the words.

'Have you got a brush? I can take the can and start working around the edges.'

The suggestion must have startled her almost as much as it startled himself, for the roller shot off across the wall at a tangent, leaving a vivid stripe of yellow on the dull and dirty green.

'You can't paint!' she protested, but whether she meant he was unable to do something so basic, or that he was too superior to dirty his hands with manual labour, he couldn't guess.

'Not only can but will,' he told her. 'In fact, I painted these walls before the clinic first opened, although I'm sure it was a more pleasant green back then. I seem to remember reading a psychological report that green was soothing, and that's why I chose it.'

He crossed the room to where he'd checked the label on the paint cans. There'd been other painting paraphernalia near them. She'd spread newspaper on the carpet, though now he looked more closely at the floor covering he realised paint splatter would probably improve it. There were two brushes, a stick for stirring, a couple of spare cloths and a small empty beetroot tin, obviously brought along so she could fill it with paint and carry it with her as she did the brushwork. He stirred the paint in the can, filled the tin and, after resealing the can, picked up the brush.

'Where's the ladder?' he asked, looking around in case he'd missed seeing it.

Jacinta turned from where she'd been determinedly rolling paint across the wall and just as determinedly ignoring him.

'I haven't got one.'

'So how were you going to do those top bits near the ceiling?'

He'd caught her out and she knew it, but she still retained considerable aplomb.

'I was going to put a chair on that small table and manage on that, but you're probably tall enough to reach just standing on a chair. I've more newspaper out the back if you want to cover the chair.'

It was at that stage Mike realised just how ridiculous this situation was. He was standing in his own waiting room, in his own clinic, being ordered around by a little snip of a woman who, as far as he was aware, had no right whatsoever to be on the premises.

But he went out the back, found the newspaper and dutifully spread it, not only on the chair but over the carpet where it abutted the wall, in case he'd lost the art of wall painting and dripped more than he should.

Tin of paint in one hand, and brush in the other, he climbed cautiously onto the chair and began to stroke the bright colour along the top of the wall. He hadn't forgotten how to do it!

'So, Jacinta who doesn't like being called Jazzy, why is the wall colour of this clinic or, for that matter, the clinic's well-being, or lack of it, your concern?'

She didn't answer immediately, and he turned to find her bent over the paint cans, refilling the tray she was using. But when she straightened she looked at him, shaking her head as if either his presence, or his personality, was beyond her understanding.

'You've no idea, have you? How many people work for you? Do you know that?'

He shrugged, thought about hazarding a guess, considered telling an outright lie and in the end shook his head, which seemed somehow better than a feeble 'no'.

'I didn't think you did,' she said, bending down to retrieve the tray, then carrying it back to the wall where she was working. 'Well, for your information, I'm one of your employees. I've even got a number to prove it—staff member four hundred and seventy-two, that's me.'

'Four hundred and seventy-two—you can't possibly be!' If he hadn't known himself better, he'd have thought he was spluttering! 'I might not know to the last digit exactly how many employees I have, but I'm damned certain it's nowhere near four hundred.'

Number four hundred and seventy-two continued to spread paint across the wall.

'I don't think you've got four hundred and seventy-two employees either.' She spoke in a kindly voice that set his teeth on edge, but she didn't falter in her task. 'I guess it's like the numbering system here, not in order.'

Mike thought back. Paul had certainly said something about a new simplified system of accounting for wages and salaries, but numbering the staff?

'That's not the point anyway,' he said, pleased to note the spluttering had lessened. 'Whatever your number, you had no right to paint the walls without permission.'

That made her turn, but only, it appeared, to smile mockingly up at him.

'Considering you're now helping me…'

Mike clenched his teeth and concentrated on getting the paint to the top of the wall without smudging the cornice.

'Only because you'd never have finished it today and I don't want either staff or patients turning up tomorrow to find the place like some graffiti artist's nightmare.'

'I'd have finished it!' Jacinta told him, although she knew she'd probably have had to work all night to do it. 'And you're not going to be much help if you stop each time you want to say something and wave the paintbrush at me like a school principal flourishing the cane!'

She sluiced the roller through the paint again, and slid it across the wall. Silence from the other side of the room told her he hadn't liked her comment, but he was probably going to fire her anyway, so it was a good time to tell him some home truths. She was marshalling her thoughts—or trying to get them off the appealing contours of his bare chest—when he beat her into speech.

'That's a ridiculously fanciful metaphor. I was merely using the brush for emphasis. Besides, school principals no longer use canes—they went out with the ark.'

Mike was aware this wasn't the conversation he should be having. He needed to know exactly who she was and what right she had to be painting his clinic, but every time he glanced her way she seemed to be reaching up to get paint to the highest possible point, an action which tightened her jeans against extremely neat buttocks and lifted her shirt so a bit of bare midriff was revealed.

Hardly the sexiest sight in the world, but distracting, nonetheless.

He tried harder.

'Can we get back to what your role is here? And just what right you have to be painting these walls?'

Skin flashed into view again, but Jacinta remained stubbornly focused on the wall as she answered him.

'I thought you said yes when I asked about painting,'

Jacinta said, though she knew he hadn't, not exactly, and he probably knew he hadn't also—not exactly!

She wanted to turn around because if she could see his face, she might be able to gauge his mood, but his face was just above that bare chest…

Mike remembered that paint had been mentioned—he'd connected it with artwork, which wasn't so surprising, given where they'd been. Maybe he had said yes, but that didn't explain *why* she was doing it.

He watched faded, paint-splashed denim tighten over the pert buttocks as she again bent to scoop paint onto the roller, then, shamed by his interest, asked her why.

'I'm doing it because I work in this clinic and I happen to think the work I do is worthwhile. I think the clinic is worthwhile, too, but it's being allowed to die—or maybe it's being killed off.'

She turned towards him now, dark eyes scanning his face, perhaps to see if she could read a murderous guilt in it. But far from arousing ire in him, her words had shocked him— no, more than that, rocked him. How long ago had he lost track of what was going on in his own business? About what was happening at this most basic yet ultimately most important level? Since the internet project started? Or before that, when he'd begun to diversify into other fields, looking for new challenges in an effort to recapture the excitement he'd felt when he'd first set up Abbott Road?

And getting back to Abbott Road—patients by number? Mike's mind was still reeling over that one, but for some reason he couldn't explain even to himself, he felt it was important that this woman didn't realise the extent of his shock.

'What kind of employee?' He stepped off the chair, shifted it along and climbed back up, the movement reminding him of his sore toe. Added 'See a doctor' to his mental list.

'A medical one.' The words were terse.

'You're a nurse?'

Even as he asked the question he sensed it was wrong. He'd read a memo some time ago, which had explained that nurses in the clinics were no longer called nurses but were attached medical staff, or something equally ridiculous.

'You don't have nurses!' The virago came in right on cue. 'Associated medical personnel—that's what Trent Clinics have. Not that I'm one of them, anyway. Four hundred numbers, if you'd ever bothered to check out your own system, are allocated to doctors, numbers over fifty to staff working in Abbott Street. I suppose in a way it's very democratic. If the patients are nothing more than numbers, why should the doctors have names?'

Mike started to protest but she was in full flight.

'Mind you, I guess when it comes to sacking someone, it's easier to sack number two hundred and twenty than Mary Smith who, as a person, might just have three kids dependent on her income. After all, numbers aren't likely to have children.'

He'd been still assimilating the number thing—it *had* to be something to do with a wages system—when she shot this barb to lodge under his skin. This time she'd gone too far. Mike climbed off the chair again and strode across to the woman.

'If you don't like working for Trent Clinics, why don't you leave?' he demanded, brandishing the paintbrush in front of her face. 'I have no doubt the numbers are allocated purely for accounting reasons. Our human resources department has won awards for its efficiency.'

'Probably because it removed the human element from all decisions,' Jacinta muttered, although she was more intimidated than she let on with the man hovering behind her. 'Leaving the business with more *resources*! And I'm not leaving,' she added, bravado making the words more threatening than she'd intended.

'Not until I've got this place back to how it should be— probably how you intended it to be when you first started, before making money became more important than helping people.'

Uh-oh, she'd gone too far. Jacinta knew it and had drawn

back before the icy disdain in his eyes—definitely grey, steely grey—made her flinch even closer to the wall.

'I'm sorry! I shouldn't have said that.' But her stammered apology was ignored.

He turned away, strode back to the wall, climbed onto the chair and began stroking paint along the strip of wall beneath the cornice as if he'd never stopped.

He'd sack her, that's what he'd do, Mike decided. Coldly and efficiently. He'd send a memo to whoever was in charge—Chris, if the woman really was a doctor—telling him to get rid of number four hundred and seventy-two.

But he wouldn't let her see his anger—wouldn't give her the satisfaction of knowing she'd scored a direct hit.

He stepped down from the chair to shift it along and, with the tin of paint and the brush in one hand, had to haul it across the grungy carpet. Of course, given the kind of day he was having, the wretched thing's legs stuck on a join so he had to lift one side and drag it. He was doing quite well, considering the handicaps of the paint tin and brush, and his anger was still simmering nicely when his fingers slipped and the chair legs dropped. Even before one hit his shoe he knew exactly what was coming. A million red-hot needles jabbed through his toe, then twisted and ground to intensify the pain.

Someone yelled, it might have been him, and yellow paint swirled upward from the tin before splattering itself liberally over the carpet, but all Mike could think about was stopping the pain.

Jacinta reached him as he dropped the ground. Ignoring the sloshes of paint, she knelt beside him.

'What happened? Is it your heart? Where does it hurt?'

He scowled at her but kept his hands wrapped firmly around his shoe. No way was anyone going to touch it—not his shoe, his foot and *definitely not* his toe.

'You can't have broken it just by dropping a chair on it,' Jacinta told him, grabbing his hand and trying to pry his fingers loose. 'So stop being a baby and let me look at it.'

Stop being a baby? When he was in more pain than he'd

been when he'd broken three ribs in the Wests versus University game?

'Leave it alone!' he roared, but she took no notice, sliding her small-boned fingers under his then levering his away. After which he couldn't speak at all as pain ricocheted through him once again.

She'd taken off his shoe and the small cool hands now cradled his instep.

And the toe felt—slightly—better.

'Looks like gout,' she said calmly, and the words had barely registered before outrage flooded through him.

'Gout? I do not have gout. Old men have gout. Heavy drinkers have gout. I'm fit, healthy and not yet forty. *I do not have gout.* I have an ingrown toenail. What would you know about it anyway?'

He'd sounded quite mature as he'd denied the gout, but the last denial had been a bit over the top, and the final demand definitely childish.

'Because four hundred numbers signify people on your medical staff. I thought I told you that. I'm a doctor here, Dr Trent.'

'Some doctor if you can't tell the difference between an ingrown toenail and gout!' he muttered as she rested his heel very carefully on a cushion she'd dragged from another chair.

'Your toenail's not the best, but the swelling around the joint of your big toe is nothing to do with that. It's gout.'

And, having pronounced this sentence on him, she walked away.

Mike bent forward and peered at the toe. It was definitely red and swollen around the middle joint—more swollen than it had seemed this morning. But the toenail had been sore on and off for weeks, so he hadn't looked too closely, simply assuring himself he'd do something about it some time.

'Here, take these.'

He looked up to find the virago standing over him, two small white tablets in her outstretched hand.

'They're colchicine, not arsenic,' she added, naming the suppressant usually prescribed for gout. 'Here's some water.'

Jacinta thrust her other hand forward and, suspecting she might throw it at him if he didn't respond, he took the paper cup of water from her then, gingerly, the tablets.

'I can't possibly have gout,' he grumbled. 'I'm too young and I look after my diet.'

'It's more to do with heredity than diet, and passed down through your mother's genes,' she said calmly. 'You can have blood tests which will show a build-up of uric acid if you like, but the quickest test is to take the tablets at intervals during the day and if it goes away you know it's gout. If it doesn't then you've an infection in your toe that's moved to the joint and you'll probably have to have it amputated.'

She was exaggerating, of course! Well, he hoped she was. He hadn't been out of hands-on medicine for so long that antibiotics could no longer clear up a bone infection.

'But why now?' he muttered, more to himself as he tried to make sense of both the diagnosis and the situation.

'Say your toe's been sore, and then you get a bit run-down—no doubt tired from counting all your money—the urate crystals that build up in your body would go to the weakest point—the sore toe.'

The explanation was acceptable but the dig she'd got in—couldn't resist it, obviously—was more than Mike could take without retaliation.

'The money I make pays your wages,' he reminded her. 'It also supports an intensive-care bed at the children's hospital, several overseas orphans, a whole platoon of workers, not to mention the families of all my staff.'

Bad move—it would have sounded better if he'd had the number of families, but he'd already admitted to her he didn't know the number.

Numbers—they'd become a recurring theme!

Surely patients weren't called by numbers.

She had to be wrong about that.

CHAPTER THREE

MIKE swallowed the tablets with a mouthful of water, set the
cup down and very gingerly climbed to his feet. His toe
throbbed, but it was slightly better without the shoe on it so
he left it off. Jacinta had returned and was making an ineffec-
tual effort to clean up the spilt paint.

She was kneeling on the floor, as far from him as she could
get and still reach the mess. Her defensive attitude told him
she knew she'd overstepped every boundary between employee and employer, yet something in the way she moved
weakened his resolve to stay angry.

Something in the way she moved made him think thoughts
he hadn't thought for a long time—and certainly didn't want
to think now. He'd never been attracted to small neat bodies—
and had made it a policy never to get involved with staff.

'Leave it. I've an old carpet runner I can put down over it
until the carpet's replaced.'

Jacinta looked up at him, unable to believe the offer—or
the suggestion that a new carpet would follow.

'That would be wonderful,' she said, and smiled because
she meant it. Though she guessed she was still teetering on a
knife-edge as far as her job was concerned, and was still com-
pletely befuddled by the situation.

Her boss—here—in Abbott Road, painting walls, suffering
gout—and disturbing her body in a way it hadn't been disturbed since Rory Ahern, the high-jump champ, had smiled at
her in high school.

But, befuddled or not, she knew he'd offered a temporary
truce. It was up to her to accept it.

'I can give you a bottle of the tablets,' she said, as she
collected her useless cleaning cloth and began to edge back

37

towards the paint tray and roller. 'You'll need to take one every two hours, day and night, until the pain goes away or they make you sick. Of course, you probably know that—the making-you-sick part—but most people can tolerate ten, or up to fifteen, without ill effects. Of course, once they make you sick—'

She stopped, mainly because her companion was looking even more befuddled than she felt.

'I'll just get on with the painting,' she muttered. 'If I keep going I'll get it done. You don't have to help. In fact, you should rest your toe.'

He took no notice, limping across to the paint cans, refilling his small tin and limping back, then climbing, very carefully, up onto the chair.

They worked in silence for what seemed like a very long time, possibly because Jacinta was so aware of his presence in the room.

Eventually he broke the silence, asking how come she'd had tablets on hand, and she realised it probably hadn't been very long at all. He was continuing from where she'd told him she'd give him a supply. 'I understood the rule was no drugs on the premises.'

Mike covered another narrow strip of old green paint and waited for an answer. He knew the question was petty—getting his own back after he'd weakened and all but promised to replace the carpet—but if he was going to learn more about the present status of the company he ran, he may as well start now.

'No addictive drugs like codeine or morphine derivatives or methadone are kept here. We give clients scripts, which they have filled at the pharmacy next door, but non-addictive drugs, like the gout tablets, well, if a drug company rep wants to leave some samples...'

'You keep them? Is this common practice?'

It was in most medical practices but against the Trent Clinic 'rules', Jacinta knew. The reasoning was that a medical practice shouldn't put itself under obligation to a particular drug company. A principle she agreed with—in principle!

She hesitated, but not for long.

'A lot of the people who use this clinic have no money,' she said. 'I know it mightn't cost much for them to have scripts filled, but the three dollars fifty they have to pay might have been set aside for milk for their kids or a cheap evening meal.'

He could hardly argue about that—now, could he? Jacinta moved on to the third wall.

'And where do you keep these samples?'

Ice had crept back into his deep voice.

'I had a secure cabinet built in.'

She painted furiously as she muttered the words. She'd asked Carmel about using the office drug safe where emergency pain relief and other supplies were kept, but when permission had been refused she'd gone right ahead and organised her own secure cabinet. Even though she was breaking the rules, she was safeguarding the drugs she did keep on the premises.

'Where?'

Intrigue had melted some of the ice.

'I'll show you when we finish painting,' she promised, so relieved he hadn't exploded she turned to flash a smile at him. 'If we keep stopping we'll never get it done.'

So it's 'we' now? Mike thought, hiding a smile of his own. He'd already had an example of how far Dr Jacinta Ford would go if given even a hint of encouragement, so returning smiles was definitely out of the question.

He'd finished painting the strip along the cornice, filled in around the doorjamb and had begun on the back wall—where a lot of work awaited him around each of the three doors—when a loud knocking on the front door startled him enough to smudge his careful line.

'Uh-oh!'

Two simple sounds that radiated guilt.

He turned towards his fellow worker, and caught the sneaky

glance she shot him and the slight flush on her paint-smudged cheeks.

He felt his anger stir again. Not only was she here without permission, *and* keeping drugs on the premises, but she'd obviously invited someone to join her.

Probably a boyfriend.

'Well, aren't you going to let whoever it is in?' he demanded.

She set the roller down in the paint tray, straightened up, then crossed the room towards the door, halting midway to turn towards him again.

'You won't yell at them?'

'Why the hell would I yell at anyone?' The words were a little loud but he certainly wouldn't have called it a yell.

'Because you don't seem very happy about this project, but these kids, if it's who I think it is, just want to help.'

'Kids? You've got kids coming in to help?' He waved his arms in the air. 'As if adults aren't making enough mess?'

'Coming,' she called as the knocking came again, adding to Mike, 'They're big kids. Self-sufficient.'

With that—and with no thought, apparently, for her own safety should it be a knife-wielding drug addict outside—she unlocked the door.

'Hi, Jacinta! Told you we'd turn up. We worked extra hard at Ellerslie House yesterday so we could get here today. And, look, Dean managed to scrounge some material from the oddments place near McDonald's, and Fizzy thought we might be able to drape it over the chairs. Make them look better.'

Scrounge or steal? Jacinta thought but, with Michael Trent glaring disapprovingly not only at her but at the three teenagers as well, she wasn't going to ask.

'That's great, Will.' She shut the door behind them, and smiled at their expressions of approval for her new colour scheme.

'Who's the guy? Your boyfriend?'

Jacinta shook her head, then led the youngsters forward.

'Dr Trent owns this place. He's helping out.' Let him deny

it if he wished. 'Dr Trent, meet Fiona, known as Fizzy, Will and Dean. They're the Abbott Road Clinic support group.'

She hoped he hadn't heard their muttered comments when she'd mentioned who he was, and was proud of them when they stepped forward in turn and held out their hands to acknowledge her introduction.

Surprised, too, when he said, 'It's Mike, not Dr Trent.'

Mike—a short, no-nonsense name. Somehow it didn't sound at all like the millionaire owner of a string of medical clinics and sundry business interests which, she'd read, included film production companies and tourism ventures.

Not that the kids knew that.

With the formality of meetings and greetings out of the way, they backed off. Then, with their usual bursts of speed, went for the paint.

'I'll do the roller,' Will, the natural leader of the group, announced. 'Dean, you grab that other brush and help the doc cut in around the doors, and the girls can fiddle with the material on the chairs.'

As her arm was aching from her efforts with the roller, Jacinta didn't argue, simply taking the plastic bag Dean handed her and motioning Fizzy to join her at the far end of the waiting room—away from the paint.

'How are you feeling?' she asked the girl, casting a professional eye over the teenager's pretty face and seeing signs of strain.

'I get tired all the time. I'd like to stay longer at the shelter—sleep in a bit—but they've got rules about being out by nine so I can't.'

'It's not an answer because I can't offer it every day, but why don't you go and lie down on the examination couch in my office? It's not the most comfortable bed in Australia, but you can rest even if you can't sleep.'

Fizzy's blue eyes filled with tears.

'You don't mind?' she whispered, and Jacinta, ashamed that such a simple offer could mean so much to this child-woman, put her arm around her shoulders and hugged her close.

'Of course I don't mind, you goose. The door's unlocked, so off you go.'

She tipped the fabric Dean had 'scrounged' onto one of the chairs, then realised loose covers wouldn't work. But she could cut the cloth so it wrapped around the seat part, and use upholstery tacks, hammered in underneath, to secure it. The city businesses were closed on a Sunday, but she'd find an open hardware shop in a nearby suburb.

'That girl's pregnant!'

She'd been so absorbed in her calculations she hadn't heard Michael's—Mike's—approach. Now she turned and was disconcerted to find him so close, his craggy face with its sharply delineated slashes of cheekbone and stubbornly jutting chin within kissing distance, if she leaned just a little forward.

Kissing distance! You're out of your mind.

'Yes!' she said, recalling what he'd said but too bewildered by the kissing thing to expand on her agreement.

'She's only a child!'

'She's thirteen.'

'That's only twelve months older than my daughter.'

Jacinta thought back to the biographical notes on Michael Trent, which she'd read before approaching him. Daughter, Elizabeth, by first—and so far only—wife, Lauren. Now Lauren Court, having divorced this hunk for some unfathomable reason and remarried, this time to someone even wealthier than her first husband.

But knowing all this didn't help. He was looking at her as if he expected her to say something, and her mind, after throwing up the fairly useless information about the man's daughter, had shut down.

'It happens,' she said weakly, professional discretion protecting Fizzy's story.

'She's gone into one of the consulting rooms.' Mike had moved closer, no doubt so he could continue to speak softly, but his proximity was worsening the problem with her brain. Particularly as he was now close enough for her to see some blue, or maybe it was green, in eyes she'd originally labelled grey.

'It's my consulting room. I told her to go in there. She's tired, and she might have a sleep if she lies down on the examination table.'

'But you've got drugs in there—you told me so yourself. And instruments.'

'Fizzy won't touch anything,' Jacinta protested, as his suspicion released her from the spell of closeness and multicoloured eyes.

'Oh, no?'

The disbelief in the question fired Jacinta's anger.

'You're the boss! Go and see for yourself if you don't believe me,' she snapped. 'Although almost as much as a good night's sleep, that young woman needs to know someone trusts her, and you poking your head in could destroy all the weeks of work I've done in convincing her to trust me.'

Mike shook his head and looked down at the fiery little creature who was almost daring him to check on the teenager. There was another word—termagant—he thought would fit Jacinta Ford. He wasn't sure exactly what it meant, but it seemed to suit. Here she was, five feet four if she was an inch, *and* one of his employees, glaring up at him with such defiance he was tempted to...

Laugh! That was the word he needed, though two words—'kiss her'—had popped first into his head.

He returned resolutely to his painting.

Kiss her?

Last night she'd appeared reasonably attractive—neat—but today? With a knitted beanie of some kind covering her shiny hair and paint smudged liberally across her unremarkable features, she certainly wasn't a candidate for kissing. But, given the thought had surfaced, he'd better stay away—put distance between them—in case it should recur and he give in to it.

Kissing her was as ridiculous as spending a perfectly good Sunday painting the walls of this waiting room. For Pete's sake! If he'd wanted the place painted, he had contractors who'd have done it with no mess, no fuss and at practically no cost, when you considered it wasn't that big a room.

And if he sold the building, it would be demolished, so the painting was a wasted effort.

'It's, like, a good place. Like, you know, safe.'

The young man—Dean—who'd been delegated to help him work around the doors mumbled the words in what Mike recognised, from contact with the offspring of his friends, as typical male teenage-speak.

But recognising the dialect didn't help him understand the content.

'Safe? Safe for you?'

'Nah.'

Mike glanced towards the lad, certain there must be more to come, but Dean was focussed on his work, frowning in concentration as he carefully brought paint right up to the architrave around the door.

'Who, then?' Mike asked, when he decided he *had* to know more.

'Kids like Fizzy. Lots of kids.'

Kids? This Dean had to be what—as old as Libby? He wasn't as tall as she was, but boys often developed later.

Intrigued as well as puzzled, Mike persisted.

'But not for you?'

'Nah!'

Dean squatted down to take his brush-strokes to floor level, and Mike waited, sure there'd be more this time.

He wasn't disappointed.

'I don't get sick.'

Ah! So Abbott Road had gained some kind of kudos among young people and was considered 'safe'. Safe from what? Police raids?

Was employee number four hundred and seventy-two handing out more than gout tablets to her patients? He glanced around, thinking he'd better ask Jacinta right now, but she'd disappeared.

'Where did Dr Ford go?'

Dean glanced around, as if checking it was him Mike was questioning.

'Jacinta? Dunno.'

She couldn't be in one of the consulting rooms as she'd have had to walk past him and Dean. Maybe she'd gone out the back—but he could hardly go after her out there and hover outside the washroom, waiting for her to come out.

He added another note to his mental list, then realised he should have been making it a written one. Apart from 'Who is Karen?', he couldn't remember a thing he had on it.

Jacinta parked her car behind the building and rested her head on the steering-wheel. Finding some upholstery tacks had been a good excuse to escape for a while, but now she had to go back in and pretend the presence of her ultimate boss, to whom she'd been unforgivably rude several times, wasn't affecting her in any way.

She could waste a little more time finding a hammer. There was a neat pack of tools in the boot of her car—something the car manufacturers had kindly provided for her. A toolkit would have a hammer.

Of course, it didn't, but it did have a fairly hefty-looking implement she assumed was for loosening wheel nuts, should she ever be struck by an urge to change a car tyre.

If held in the right way, it would make a reasonable hammer.

'Well, that certainly makes a better weapon than a paint-roller, but I thought, as I was helping you out on this project, you might have given up the physical attack option.'

The cry she let out was more a squeak of terror than anything else. Coming from the sunlit yard into the gloom of the passage, she'd failed to see Mike, then his voice had scraped along already raw nerves.

'Don't do that!' she said, brandishing the tool at him. 'Creeping up on people! I could have died of fright.'

'It was hardly creeping up as I was in front of you,' Mike pointed out with faultless logic. Then he took in the plastic bag she was carrying and peered more closely at her face. 'Have you been out? To a shop? Looking like that?'

Jacinta bit back a groan, stiffened her spine and glared at her boss.

'I needed some upholstery tacks,' she said in her snootiest manner. 'And looks are really very unimportant in my scale of priorities.'

Having delivered this cutting rejoinder, she was about to march past him when another thought struck her.

'Not that you're in any position to comment on other people's appearances.' She did a long and very obvious survey of him, top to toe—bare and swollen—then back up again, over paint-spotted trousers, paint-splashed chest—she really must stop looking at that chest—to smudged face and...

Smiling grey eyes?

His eyes were smiling at her?

And was that slight twitch of his lips the beginnings of a lip smile? The real thing?

'Pax?' he said, using a word she hadn't heard since she'd been at school. He held out his hand.

'Pax,' she agreed, but one hand had the bag of tacks and the other the wrench, so all she could do was smile right back at him.

'Jacinta, could you come? Fizzy's sick.'

The alarm in Will's voice made her forget smiles and she rushed past Mike, heading for her consulting room.

Fizzy was indeed being sick, but the blood spreading across the sheet on the examination table was far more worrying.

Dean had found a stainless-steel basin and, though white-faced with horror and probably his own nausea, was grimly holding it in front of Fizzy as she retched and moaned.

'Spontaneous abortion,' Jacinta muttered to Mike, who'd followed her into the room. 'It will be quicker to drive her to the hospital than wait for an ambulance. Could you take Dean outside while I do what I can here? Then I'll get you and the boys to carry her out to the car.'

Mike reacted to the urgency in her voice, touching Dean lightly on the shoulder then guiding him towards the door.

'Go and tip that out and rinse out the bowl. She might need it in the car,' he told the still shaken lad.

He turned to Will.

'I'll drive so Jacinta can look after Fizzy. Can you two guys keep going with the painting?'

He must be mad—he knew that. He'd figured out by now the three were most likely street kids. And to leave two of them here, unsupervised, in a medical clinic? The doors to the reception area and the other two consulting rooms might be locked, but these kids could probably pick a lock faster than he could use a key.

'Mike, we're ready. My car's out the back—that's the easiest way.'

Jacinta's voice reminded him of the first priority—getting Fizzy to the hospital.

'I can carry her on my own,' he added to Will. 'Could you go on ahead and open the back door of the car? Get the basin from Dean on the way. I'll get back to finish the painting as soon as I can.'

Fizzy was swathed in a coat and a blanket but still shivering from either blood loss or shock.

'I've started a saline drip but didn't want to give her anything else until a specialist has seen her.'

Jacinta was holding the bag of saline in her hand and, though undoubtedly the scruffiest doctor he'd seen in some time, looked efficient and in control.

'I'll walk beside you so we don't pull out the catheter.'

He lifted the girl, so light she might have been an infant, and made his way swiftly across the waiting room, down the passage and out into the yard. Both boys were hovering anxiously by the car.

'She'll be OK,' Jacinta assured them. 'She'll probably lose the baby but when this happens it usually means there was something wrong with it and it wouldn't have survived anyway. It's not something doctors can predict and it's nobody's fault. All we have to think about is getting Fizzy well again.'

She glanced towards Mike who'd settled Fizzy in the back seat of her car. He'd think her totally irresponsible if she left Will and Dean on their own in the clinic, yet if she suggested they leave because she had to lock the place she'd be destroying a lot of the trust she'd so painstakingly built up between them.

Indecision joined her urgency and she felt a momentary rush of panic.

'I told the lads I'd get back to give them a hand as soon as I've dropped you off.'

Mike's words were so unexpected, so startling, that Jacinta suspected her jaw had dropped.

'In you get,' he added. 'We've got to get going.'

He walked around to the driver's door, held out his hand for the car keys and nodded to the boys.

'Shut and lock the back door behind you when you go back in,' he said to them. 'You don't know what weirdos might be hanging around these back alleys.'

He started the car and reversed expertly out of the back yard.

'I assume we're going to the Royal Women's,' he said.

Fizzy protested as Jacinta agreed with the destination.

'We have to go there, love,' she said gently, wrapping her arm around Fizzy and holding her tight. 'You need proper care, care that I can't give you. You'll have an ultrasound and the specialist will check what's happening. If they can't save the baby, you may need a minor operation to clean things out. I can't do it in the surgery, Fizzy, but I'll be there for you and you can come to my place when you're ready to come out. We'll give that as your address. I'll say you're my ward. We'll work it out.'

She was so intent on offering comfort to the distraught girl that she failed to consider what effect her words were having on their chauffeur. But though he'd said he was going back to the clinic to help the boys, when Fizzy had been taken to

Theatre and Jacinta had completed all the booking formalities, he was right there, in the waiting room.

Waiting!

'You'll say she's your ward? You've given false information to the hospital authorities? Are you mad?'

The deep voice, though muted to a gruff whisper, was still powerful and Jacinta glanced around.

'Hush!' she muttered at him. 'Anyway, you should be gone. Those boys are on their own and the painting will never get finished. I'll walk out to the car with you and explain.'

He muttered something that sounded like, 'You'd better,' but Jacinta was too busy working out what she could and couldn't tell to take much notice of the threat.

'It wasn't false information.' That was obviously the best place to start if she wanted to rid him of the suspicion she was a liar as well as a fool. 'I told them to put me down as the contact person and that I'd take responsibility for her.'

'Why?'

They were outside the main doors of the hospital now, and Jacinta was surprised to see the sun still high in the sky. The day seemed to have been going on for ever.

'Because she doesn't want any contact with her own family and, as she's a minor, the hospital would be obliged to make an effort to get in touch with them. But now I've gone guarantor, so to speak, the hospital won't bother—or they shouldn't. Not for a day or so and by that time she'll be out.'

She saw Mike frown and knew he was about to ask why again.

'Look, I've got to get back in there in case Fizzy needs me, and you told the boys you'd be back. There's a back-door key on my car key ring.' She scrabbled in her handbag which she'd grabbed as they'd left the consulting room. 'Here's ten dollars. Get them some junk food for lunch, would you? They're probably starving and won't be able to leave the place because they haven't got keys to get back in.'

She thrust the note into his hand and fled.

Mike watched her disappear back through the front entrance. He fancied he could still see the flashes of yellow paint on her jeans long after she'd disappeared into the gloom. Him with no shirt and no shoe and her covered in paint, they'd made a good pair as they'd walked into A and E.

A good pair?

He looked down at the ten-dollar note she'd shoved at him. He had the fanciful notion he'd been sucked into a whirlpool, spinning around and around in a situation over which he had absolutely no control.

Which was ridiculous, because if there was one thing he prided himself on, it was control. Control of his life, his business, his emotions.

Though maybe he couldn't be one hundred per cent certain about the business part of that statement right now, but that was because he'd been so involved in setting up the medical site on the internet and going into all the ramifications of providing a medical service by remote control.

But because he was a controlled kind of person, he could soon fill in the missing gaps.

Thus assured, slightly, he made his way back to Jacinta's car, folded himself into a seat built for midgets and tried to work out where he'd find a junk-food outlet. Preferably one with a drive-through service counter so he didn't have to extricate himself from the car an extra time.

CHAPTER FOUR

THE sun had finally gone down when Jacinta left the hospital. Fizzy was resting comfortably and had been persuaded to stay in overnight, but only after Jacinta had rung the clinic and asked Mike to despatch Will and Dean to the hospital.

Now that the two boys were there, and had promised to stay until visiting hours were over, Jacinta was free to finish the job she'd started, however many hours ago it had been. At least Mike wouldn't be there. According to the boys, they'd completed the painting then he'd driven them to the hospital in her car. He'd left it in the parking area with instructions to the boys to give her the keys, and had taken a cab, presumably back to his own car and then home.

She found the car, drove back to town and parked behind the clinic, glad of the security light her arrival activated. Unlocking the back door, she snapped on the lights in the passage and disarmed the alarm. The smell of paint was over-whelming. Hopefully it might dissipate a little by morning, or nauseous patients would regret coming in.

Another key opened the door to the waiting room, but this time she didn't need to switch on any lights. They were on and what they revealed made her catch her breath in surprise.

'I'm glad you came back. The security firm didn't give me a key for any internal doors so if I needed a bathroom before I finished, I was going to have to find one up in the mall.'

Mike was at the far end of the room, an upended chair balanced on the floor in front of him.

'Y-you came b-back?' Jacinta stuttered. 'Why?'

'Same reason you did, I suppose. To finish the job.' He waved his hand around in the air. 'What do you think?'

51

But Jacinta was still taking in the man rather than the room. Thankfully, he was once again wearing a shirt.

And an old slipper with the toe cut out on his left foot.

Guilt smote her!

'I'm sorry. I didn't give you more tablets!' she said. 'If you'd kept taking them it would have been feeling better by now.'

'It is feeling better now, thank you. Slightly better.' His smile would have disarmed a terrorist! 'I stopped at a friendly pharmacy on the way back from the hospital, showed ID and swore on a stack of pharmacology books I'd return with a completed script, then flashed my toe and got some tablets.'

'I'll write you a script now,' she said, glad of something to do—something that would take her, even momentarily, out of the room, so she'd stop staring at him.

And remembering the smile.

'You haven't told me what you think.'

His voice stopped her escape and she turned, and this time did look around.

'You've been doing the chairs,' she said, although it seemed totally unbelievable that such a thing could be happening. *She* might have covered chairs to make the waiting room look better, but Michael Trent, should he have wanted the place looking better, could have ordered a dozen new chairs—two dozen, in fact, or twenty dozen. Michael Trent tacking suspect lengths of material over the old chairs? It simply didn't make sense.

'It looks fantastic,' she said, because he seemed to be waiting for an answer, and because it did. As good as his word, he'd found a carpet runner which covered the worst of the paint stains, all the old green walls were now bright yellow and stacked against the end wall were what looked like a number of paintings or prints.

He must have seen her looking at them.

'I thought, with such smart new walls, it would be a shame to put back the old posters of diseased lungs and immunisation schedules. We can put them in the consulting rooms, if you think patients need to see them, and hang a few cheerful pictures on the wall.'

'Cross-sections of warts, I suppose?' Jacinta teased. She'd been so bemused by his use of the pronoun 'we' it was a wonder she could talk at all.

He chuckled at her remark, and the deep, seductive sound restarted the tingle, only this time it wasn't just in her stomach. It was in her skin, and in her chest, and down her arms and legs, and causing the curl thing again in her toes.

'I'll get you a script,' she said, and hurried as fast as she could, without actually running, towards her consulting room.

Mike watched her scuttle—there was no other word for it—away, and wondered what he'd done to bother her. He hadn't expected extravagant praise for his efforts and she'd finally offered the word 'fantastic', but only after he'd prompted her, and even then it had lacked a good deal in the heartfelt department.

Put out by her reaction, he attacked the next tack with unnecessary gusto, driving it into his forefinger instead of the chair.

Cursing his clumsiness—and the woman who'd suckered him into this job—he sucked at the blood, then realised it gave him a perfect excuse to follow her into her consulting room. Someone who kept a private supply of drugs—against the clinic rules—would doubtless be able to supply a sticky plaster.

She was over by the sink, rubbing a small hand towel across her face, a very disconcerting action from his point of view.

'You haven't been crying, have you?'

Warm brown eyes peered at him across the top of the towel.

'Crying? Why on earth would I be crying? I've been running around all day with paint on my face—you told me so, remember—so I thought I'd wash it off.'

Jacinta was pleased the excuse sounded so reasonable. She could hardly have told him that splashing her face with cold water had been an attempt to cure the tingles.

And it hadn't worked.

First his voice, accusing though it had been, then the sight of him, had brought them back a thousandfold.

She was battling the renewed attack when she saw the blood on the snowy white handkerchief he held in his hand.

'Oh, heavens, I thought we'd finished with blood for the day.'

Setting all thoughts of tingles firmly aside, she crossed the room and took his hand in hers. Seeing the tiny pinprick, she shook her head.

'You must have squeezed it to make so much blood come out. Is that why you came in? Do you need a plaster to make it better? Plain or coloured? I can even do a cartoon one, if I've any left. Barney Rubble or Fred Flintstone?'

Jacinta looked up at him, not really expecting a reply, and saw something in the grey-green, or possibly grey-blue now, of his eyes that stopped both the tingles and her breath. She was still holding his hand—couldn't bring herself to release it—and her brain had stopped working.

Also her lungs.

And possibly her heart.

'Fred Flintstone, if you've got one,' he said, his voice huskier than a forty-a-day smoker's.

It should have restarted normal functioning within her body, but the huskiness added to her confusion, so in the end Mike gently withdrew his hand and stepped away from her, breaking the spell he'd cast upon her.

Unwittingly, she hoped as she scrabbled through a drawer for the particular dressing she'd offered him. The man would be lethal if he could affect women like that at will!

'How did you leave things with Fizzy?' he asked as she ripped the protective paper off the dressing and steeled herself to approach—to touch—him again.

'She was still a little dopy from the operation. The obstetrician did a D and C straight away as she was still bleeding quite severely, but she'll be OK.'

'Upset?'

She had taken his hand again so had to look up into his

eyes. He seemed genuinely concerned and she set aside her preconceived notion of Michael Trent the cold-blooded corporate boss and responded to his expression.

'I don't know,' she said slowly, sticking the little bit of plaster around his finger then releasing his hand so she could step away from him again.

'I think in time she'll be relieved, but she was on her own— on the streets—because she refused to have an abortion.'

Jacinta hesitated. How much could she tell him—and how much did he really want to know?

But Fizzy was one of the patients who'd convinced her of the need for Abbott Road to stay open, so maybe Fizzy's story would help.

'Let's get back to the upholstery work. I'll explain as we tack. If I don't get some food soon I'll collapse.'

He started to say something about going out for food, but she waved his protests away.

'Finish the chairs first, then food, then I really should get back to the hospital. I want to see her before I go home.'

'You're a bossy little thing,' he grumbled as he followed her out of the room, but Jacinta didn't mind the insult. She was glad to be in the bigger space, where the power of Mike's presence should be lessened by the space she could put between them.

And if she focussed on what she had to do…

Hard when the man was smiling at her as he organised the task.

'Four chairs left, that's two each, though I've got it down to such a fine art I'll probably beat you. And I'll let you use my hammer. I managed with the wrench until I took the boys up to the hospital, then I slipped home for a hammer.'

Mike passed her the hammer, a piece of material and a handful of tacks.

'I've figured the secret is in doing one side first then pulling the material really tightly across the seat and holding it with two tacks on the other side while you get the rest of it right.

The underside isn't too neat but I don't suppose many of our patients pick up the chairs to check the underneath.'

Did he sound as uneasy as he felt?

Or was the feeling more unsettled than uneasy?

And why should *he* feel uneasy? Or unsettled? Apart from the fact that this was his clinic—and these were his chairs— he was doing this woman a favour!

He glanced towards Jacinta, and saw the pink tip of her tongue held between her teeth as she hammered the first tack home. Her face might now be free of paint, but her clothes were still a disgrace, yet that pink tongue-tip, and the way her shiny brown hair, released from the protective cap, now fell softly to her shoulders, attracted his attention.

Attracted him?

'You were going to tell me about Fizzy,' he reminded her, and saw the tongue-tip disappear and a frown appear between her eyes as she glanced, briefly, his way.

'She wanted the baby,' she said, returning to work and hammering fiercely. 'I suppose that translates to wanting someone to love—having someone of her own. Without understanding the reality of motherhood, the idea of a baby of their very own is very seductive for an unloved and abused young woman.'

'Abused?'

He must have revealed a healthy dose of scepticism in the word for Jacinta flashed another frown his way.

'She became pregnant by her stepfather. His abuse had been going on for years—which is why she finds it hard to sleep at night. She'd lie awake expecting—dreading—his arrival in her room. When she was younger, he told her he'd kill her if she told anyone, and he was—is—a violent enough man for her to believe him. When she did finally tell her mother, her step-father, naturally, denied it and it was Fizzy's word against his.'

Mike felt physically sickened by the story Jacinta was re-laying in flat, unemotional tones. Stories of childhood abuse appeared in newspapers so often these days he'd begun to wonder if all of them were true, or if digging into the past, for some people, might be a way of excusing their behaviour in the present.

But he'd met Fizzy, and what had happened to her wasn't far enough in the past to be a distorted memory. What had happened to her—as far as the pregnancy was concerned anyway—was real.

'But once she was pregnant? Surely then her mother must have accepted it?'

'Why?'

Jacinta finished the chair she'd been working on, set it back on its legs and turned to look at him.

'Because she's her mother?' she answered for him. 'Do you think a woman who's sworn to love, honour and cherish the man she married wants to believe he's been raping her daughter—because that's what it is. We call it abuse, and people think, Oh, so he yelled at her occasionally—but what's been going on with that child is rape. He's been raping her—regularly—and because her mother couldn't handle that concept, she accused Fizzy of lying, of deceit and of promiscuity.'

She paused because her voice was shaking with the rage Fizzy's story always caused and she didn't want to make a complete fool of herself.

'Then her mother kicked her out. Thirteen, pregnant and out on the streets. Will and Dean found her on her second night and more or less adopted her. They'd been on their own for a while and knew the shelters and how to get youth allowance, but they also knew she should have some kind of regular medical attention so eventually they took her to the Women's Hospital. The sister who saw her first contacted social workers, who contacted her mother, who labelled her a runaway and took her home, where her stepfather belted her black and blue in the hope of causing a miscarriage.'

The loud oath from Mike told her what effect her story was having on him, and she looked up to see him shaking his head in disbelief.

'We read about it,' she said gently, trying to ease the physical revulsion she knew he was feeling, 'see people talking about it on TV, but somehow we're so inured to it we tend to cope with the concept of adults' cruelty and misuse of children by not thinking too much about it, by telling ourselves it's rare and the authorities are probably handling it.'

Mike nodded but didn't say anything, so she hammered in tacks on the second chair, the sharp blows punctuating the words as she finished her story.

'The boys saw her home address on the hospital form she filled out. They went to the house, guessing what was likely to happen. Fizzy came out at three in the morning, barely able to walk. The boys got her to a corner store where there's a phone, rang me and I picked all three of them up and took them home.'

'How come they had your number? Why would they ring you?'

'Last one done,' she said, tipping it up, then looking at the unfinished chair he had tipped upside down but wasn't working on. 'Here, use the hammer. You're holding up the show.'

He took the hammer, but not the hint.

'Why you?' he repeated.

'I'd met them before—the boys—and told them to ring if ever they were in trouble and needed me. I'd given them a phone card to use, so as long as they could find a public phone they'd be right.'

Mike hammered the last of the tacks into place. Fizzy's story had sickened him, and he knew there was more to Jacinta's tale of 'meeting' Will and Dean, but he'd heard the exhaustion in her voice and didn't want to push for more.

Hell! He was exhausted himself, and he'd arrived hours after she'd begun the painting. And on top of the physical work, she'd had all the emotional stress of Fizzy's miscarriage.

'All done,' he announced. 'Now, tell me which painting you want where and I'll get them hung. Then I'll take you out to dinner before you go to the hospital.'

'You don't need to take me out to dinner,' she protested, and he smiled to himself. Ninety-nine point nine per cent of the women he knew would have used paint-stained jeans as an excuse, but Jacinta seemed to have as little regard for her appearance as she did for his opinion of her.

'I know that, but we both need to eat and there's a little wine bar up the road that used to have fantastic food. I know it's still there because I parked my car near it and walked down the mall. I'd like to revisit it, and don't want to eat alone.'

To him, this explanation was eminently reasonable—and it was, more or less, the truth. He did know the place, and the food had been good, and spending a little more time in Jacinta's company made good business sense.

Wanting to spend more time in her company was a matter he'd consider later.

But in spite of all this reasonable reasoning, the look she'd shot at him while he'd contemplated his own incentives had been chock-full of suspicion.

'If you mean Marco's, the food's still good, but he closes at nine on Sunday nights. If you want to eat there we'll have to go now and hang the paintings later.'

'I know you want to go back to the hospital so I can hang the paintings later,' he heard himself offer. It wasn't a whirlpool he was in but quicksand—and he was being sucked in deeper and deeper by the minute. Yet he found himself adding, with almost cheerful aplomb, 'At least, once the nails are in place, you can change them around if they don't suit.'

The second look he got had disbelief mixed with the suspicion, but Jacinta walked across to her consulting room and ducked inside. Within seconds he heard water running.

He'd won! She was coming to dinner with him.

Mike cooled his unexpected spurt of satisfaction by reminding himself she was coming to eat with him because she was hungry and in no way did she see this as anything more than convenience.

'I'll check the back is locked and set the alarm,' she said a few minutes later, locking the door of the consulting room and turning to face him, the brown hair, brushed into shining submission, falling like dark silk around her face. 'It's easier to leave my car here and walk back for it later.'

She disappeared out the door, which was when he realised that instead of staring after her, thinking about dark silk, he should be following to wash his hands and check his own features for paint blobs before she locked the interior door.

Jacinta spent the time away from him lecturing herself on the fact that eating with Mike was an opportunity to tell him all that was wrong at Abbott Road—things that needed more than paint to fix. She was *not* to blow it by mooning over the man, or being distracted by eyes that were as changeable in colour as lake water. Neither would she be seduced into forgetting what was, after all, a duty by a voice that raised goose-bumps on her arms and caused stomach tingles just thinking about it.

Concentrating on this lecture to herself, even nodding her own agreement to each of her own points, it meant she wasn't looking where she was going, so she walked full tilt into Mike as he emerged from the bathroom.

Then they did that silly thing people did when walking towards each other on the street—both went one way, then the other, until in the end he seized her gently by the upper arms and steered her around his body.

She was busy rubbing her arms to get rid of more goosebumps when she heard his low, alluring chuckle.

'Would you believe I'm going the wrong way now?' He'd turned to follow her back to the waiting room. 'All I was going to do was check you'd finished locking up.'

But Jacinta wasn't going to be distracted by low alluring chuckles. As if the tingles weren't enough, the goose-bumps had been a pretty good indication that spending time with this man was the folliest of follies—if follies came in degrees. Sure, there were things she needed to discuss, but now she'd met him she could get through to him on the phone—

No! Phones meant voices and his voice was part of the problem.

Surely her emails would get to him now they'd met. He must have—

She turned towards him.

'Do you have a private email address?'

'Trying to duck out of dinner, Jacinta?' he asked, as if her motive were lit by a neon sign above her head. 'My email address won't do you any good. I'm not at home or at the office to collect a polite sorry-but-I-can't-make-it email.'

Jacinta managed to look affronted—or hoped it was affronted she looked, not plain foolish!

Tried for dignity.

'I was asking so I could let you know how Fizzy gets on.' Had 'blatant lie' popped into the signboard above her head? 'From past experience, emails addressed to you at head office fail to get through.'

She whisked out the front door, then realised she'd forgotten to arm the alarm and whisked back in again—bumping into the man for the second time in five minutes.

'Seems I'm always getting in your way,' he said, the deep voice stroking her nerves while his hands, resting again on her upper arms to steady her, set fire to her skin.

'No, no! It was my fault. Not looking where I'm going. Not expecting anyone else to be here after hours.'

She was rambling, but that was only because Mike still had hold of her and, though totally impersonal, his touch was destroying whatever remnants of equilibrium she'd retained after this most confusing and emotional day.

'But you are?'

Jacinta frowned up at him.

Are what? Couldn't he hear?

'Here after hours?' he clarified, a slight pucker of the skin between his eyebrows threatening imminent disapproval.

'Not often. Paperwork. You know.'

She tried for airy nonchalance and would have been more successful if he hadn't still been holding her and she'd been able to step away from him—wave her arms about a bit.

Suspicion warred with a feeling Mike didn't want to name. Calling it attraction would be ridiculous. He was intrigued by the woman, nothing more. And paperwork was a reasonable reason to work late—so why did she seem so wary about admitting it?

And he should let go of her, no matter how warm and velvety to the touch her skin might seem.

He forced his fingers loose.

'Sorry,' he muttered when he saw red marks on her arms where his hands had been. 'I keep grabbing you, but it's self-preservation—fear you might accidentally step on my toe.'

He hoped he didn't sound as if he was mumbling—the words had seemed a bit uncertain in his head.

'That's OK,' Jacinta said, so sweetly he wondered if he'd imagined the virago. 'Why don't you go on up the steps so there's no possibility of an accident? I'll stay here, set the alarm, lock up and then follow. It *is* a narrow stairway.'

Was she making excuses for him or teasing him? Mike wasn't sure, but the suggestion was sensible, particularly as it removed him from Jacinta's immediate vicinity on a temporary basis at least. He climbed the stairs, aware the dim light was all the entrance offered. He added 'Better lighting' to the list he kept forgetting to write down.

Maybe he was losing it.

He could see the headlines now. BUSINESS MAGNATE BURNT OUT AT THIRTY-EIGHT! CLINIC EMPIRE COLLAPSES.

'I don't suppose you know who Karen is?' he said gloomily, when Jacinta joined him and they turned towards the wine bar.

'Karen in your office? The one who's just had the baby? Actually, I popped in to see her for a minute while I was at the hospital. Saw the baby, too! He's a gorgeous little boy.'

She sighed as if seeing a baby was the most blissful occurrence in the world.

'Does she handle your emails? Is that why you asked?'

Jacinta stopped walking and turned to frown at him.

'Oh, no, that can't be right. I know she'd pass on anything I sent to her. She's been to Abbott Road herself—when her husband jammed his thumb in the car door and she came to pick him up because he couldn't drive. Fainted at the sight of blood, poor man. Karen was sure he'd pass out during the delivery, but apparently he came through like a trouper.'

Mike folded his lips tightly together and gritted his teeth so he didn't say anything stupid, but if he'd been disconcerted earlier about some of the things he didn't know about his employees—about his business, in fact—he was now furious. Here was this woman, employed to be a doctor, nothing else, prattling on about someone who worked in *his* office, miles from the city, as if they were second-best friends. She not only knew who Karen was, but apparently knew Karen's entire family!

If he could just place this Karen…

He closed his eyes and tried to visualise the staff in the big room he occasionally walked through on his way to see Barry or Chris or Jill. Could he see anyone in the picture with a bulging stomach?

'Yow! Hell!'

He was vaguely aware of Jacinta starting as he yelled, but the pain in his toe was so excruciating he couldn't worry about startling someone. He slumped onto the wrought-iron seat someone had placed practically in the middle of the mall, its legs at such an angle that any unsuspecting passer-by could stub his toe on it.

'You must have seen it!' Jacinta said, and he could hardly tell her about the red haze of anger, or about closing his eyes as he'd tried to picture Karen.

'Well, I didn't,' he snapped, his hands clutching his slipper while the fire in his toe diminished slightly.

'Did you take another tablet?'

Of course he hadn't. He'd taken one at two, then one at four, but he'd been so busy, covering chairs, that six o'clock had come and gone.

'Are they in your pocket? You can take one now. I can slip back to the clinic and get you some water. Then you should go home. Going to the wine bar was a silly idea when you're in so much pain. What if someone trod on it?'

Going home was a sensible suggestion but he knew if he

didn't get answers to at least some of the questions this unusual day had thrown up, he would go mad.

He didn't need *all* the answers, just some.

He wouldn't ask anything more about Karen. He wasn't about to admit to not knowing one of his own office staff. However, there were questions about Fizzy and the boys, and about Jacinta's deliberately offhand reply to his question about her after-hours activities and, now he thought about it, he wouldn't mind knowing if Adam Lockyer *was* her boyfriend.

'We'll go to the wine bar,' he said. Telling himself his mind could conquer pain, he put his foot gingerly to the ground and tested it by putting weight on it.

'Actually, it's no worse than it was before,' he said, surprised into admitting it. 'Apparently it's only when it hits something that it really hurts.'

Jacinta's look suggested she didn't believe a word he was saying, but she didn't argue with him, though she did offer a hand to help him to his feet.

And he took it, not because he needed it but because he'd remembered just how small and fragile her hand had felt in his the previous evening, and he wanted to know if he'd imagined it.

He hadn't, so he kept hold of it, pleased she didn't try to pull it away.

Walking hand in hand with him is not a good idea, Jacinta told herself, but she was tired and it had been an emotional day, and to have someone to hold her hand was very comforting.

Or it would have been, if the hand holding hers wasn't causing other problems—offering things that went far, far beyond comfort.

CHAPTER FIVE

THEY reached the wine bar, where Marco greeted Jacinta so warmly she thought maybe she didn't look as disreputable as she'd imagined she did.

'And Mike,' he said, putting out both hands to clasp Mike's with warm enthusiasm. 'So many years we don't see you here. You and Lauren, you do all your courting here and then don't come back. She is well, your lovely lady?'

Jacinta did another uh-oh, though mentally this time, and looked at Mike to see how he'd handle it.

'Very well,' Mike said smoothly, 'though she's no longer mine. We parted ways six years ago, Marco.'

Was Marco thrown by this information?

No way.

In fact, he seemed pleased, turning to beam at Jacinta.

'So now he comes with you, little one. That is good, no?'

'We've been working down at the clinic—painting the walls in case you couldn't guess—and need to eat, Marco. That's the extent of the "with me" thing!'

'You didn't have to sound quite so negative about being with me,' Mike complained, when Marco had bustled off to fix drinks and get a blackboard menu for them.

'Considering it's Marco, I probably didn't sound negative enough. I don't know what he was like back when you were courting your wife, but I only have to nod at a man I know, usually a patient, and he's trying to marry me off to him. Marco's a born matchmaker, and anyone wanting to steer clear of attachments should steer clear of him.'

She slipped onto a stool, which made her feel slightly taller, but she'd need to be ten feet to be able to handle this situation with anything even close to aplomb. First she'd let him hold

her hand—hadn't made the slightest effort to withdraw it—
and now Marco was making suggestive remarks.

And Michael Trent was going to start asking questions she
didn't want to have to answer.

Mike studied her for a moment. She'd slipped onto the stool
with the smooth movements of a woman at ease with her
body—and with the image she portrayed. She'd spoken to
Marco with genuine affection, but no hint of flirtation. In fact,
there was no artifice at all in Jacinta—or none that he'd ob-
served.

She didn't even appear to be perturbed by the silence which
had fallen between them. Certainly hadn't rushed to fill it.
Once again he had to search back through his mind to find
what they'd been talking about, but when he replayed her
words in his head, a new question arose. One which, for some
unfathomable reason, bothered him.

'Why do you want to steer clear of attachments?' he asked.

She turned to him with a hint of amusement in her dark
eyes, and he suspected he could hear a gurgle of laughter in
her voice as she replied.

'I was thinking about you when I said steer clear of Marco.
I did some research on the big boss before I found you near
the wart painting, and just about every article I read made it
very clear that, as far as you were concerned, one marriage
was enough for a lifetime.'

'When you consider the high cost of divorce and the damage extensive settlement payments can do to a business, it
should be enough for anyone,' he told her—lectured her
maybe—but, considering the disruption this woman had already caused in his life, it was best she understood his feelings
on marriage.

'I'm not blaming Lauren,' he continued, pleased he could
now—finally—discuss his divorce in calm, rational tones. 'She
encouraged me to expand into more than one clinic and was
entitled to her share, but paying her out put a severe strain on
the company's viability for a few years. When you've worked
for years to establish financial security, not only for yourself

and your own family but for a lot of friends and colleagues and their families, you have to think carefully before putting it all in jeopardy.'

'So you can't afford a new wife in case things go wrong again? Isn't that rather a defeatist attitude? Wouldn't you be better working on the assumption that next time it will work out?'

Mike frowned at his companion.

'Why should it?' he demanded, and was going to point out that just as success could breed success, so failure could breed failure, when he caught sight of his companion's ringless fingers. 'And you're what—twenty-six, -seven? And apparently not committed. So what gives you the right to lecture me on marriage?'

'I'm thirty and at least I'm honest enough to admit I'm too involved with my work to have time for a relationship,' she retorted. 'Right now, with everything that's happening, it wouldn't be fair to any partner, who'd only get the scraps of my attention.' She hesitated, then the brown eyes looked candidly into his and she added, 'Though, to be honest, there's more to it than that. My parents had a wonderful marriage— the love they shared was obvious to everyone. It shone and glittered like crystals in sunlight. So, somehow, I grew up expecting it would happen to me and I waited for it—for the gut-wrenching, heart-seizing, breath-taking advent of love. It never came. I didn't ever feel that way about a man so, rather than settle for second best...'

'You threw yourself into good works.'

The soft eyes hardened.

'I did no such thing. I just happen to believe there's more to medicine than handing out pills and potions. And that doctors in general practice are in the perfect position to help with community problems.'

She sighed, and her voice softened again as she added, 'There's so much to do, Mike, to help kids like Dean and Will and Fizzy, and that's just one area of concern.'

Once again he heard the commitment in her voice, and wondered where, along the line, he'd lost his own inner fire. He'd found challenges in expansion, in diversifying, but, as today had proved, in so doing he'd lost touch with where and what he'd started. Lost touch with the people who worked for him. Was that why the fire was gone?

He was pondering this when Marco arrived with a light beer for him and a glass of wine for Jacinta, and began his explanation of the featured dishes.

By the time they'd ordered, Mike had forgotten what they'd been discussing—again—mainly because even while deciding between a smoked salmon and avocado sauce or a tomato, olive and anchovy sauce on her penne, Jacinta had poked that little tip of pink tongue between her teeth, and he'd had a sudden flight of fancy about that tongue-tip touching his— perhaps exploring other parts of his body as well.

You don't get involved with staff, he reminded himself, so even if she was your type, which she isn't, she'd be off limits. He tried harder to recall the conversation, then remembered an earlier unfinished one and grasped it.

'Fizzy and the boys. You were going to tell me more about them.'

'Deliberate change in conversation, Dr Trent?' she said. 'A switch to something less provocative?'

Provocative? Damn it all! What *had* they been discussing?

'However, since you ask, I met Will not long after I started work at the clinic. I'd been working late one night and when I went out to my car I found the security lights weren't working and I all but fell over him.'

'He was sleeping in the back yard? In the car park of the clinic? He could have been run over if someone had driven in late at night.'

Jacinta sipped at her wine, then smiled at him.

'He wasn't sleeping there, but looking for someone he thought might be using the place to doss down. He's got a very over-developed sense of responsibility and apparently one of the younger kids hadn't turned up at the shelter that night and Will had gone out looking for him.'

Mike shook his head, unable to assimilate the thought of these youngsters, many of them still children, fending for themselves on the street.

'So I helped him look.'

She made it sound as if it was a normal thing to do—to walk around back alleys with a street kid she'd only just met! Mike was about to protest, when she continued.

'We went on foot first, all around the city centre, then took my car and drove around the parks and outer edges of the city. He was near a bar down the end of Ransome Street, prepared to sell himself for a feed.'

'Or drugs?'

Jacinta nodded, the smile gone and a look of such sadness on her face Mike reached out and rested his hand on her shoulder.

'Or drugs,' she admitted. 'Twelve years old and already addicted. He died a couple of weeks later. By then Will and I were friends, and Dean had joined us in our nightly patrols. They were both clean—free of drugs—and Dean admired the way Will took care not only of the younger kids but of older ones who needed help.'

'They're how old, those two boys?'

She smiled again but shifted slightly so that his hand slid away.

'Dean's fifteen, Will fourteen. They're both small for their age.'

She didn't have to explain why. Malnourishment was the most obvious cause of a child failing to thrive.

'And do you still patrol the streets with them?'

Jacinta studied him for a moment. Did he really want to know or was he just making conversation?

'Sometimes,' she admitted. 'They're more organised now and have a roster of people who help. Volunteers can phone the different youth shelters to see if any of their regulars haven't turned up. The shelters share information better, so the volunteers know where to look. Will and Dean still take their turns and that's how they found Fizzy. They were looking for someone else.'

'But overnight shelter isn't enough for these kids!' Mike protested, and Jacinta beamed at him, diverting his mind, momentarily, from the explanation.

'Of course it isn't. It's a stop-gap measure, but it's a starting point as well. The shelters have heaps of information they give out. Kids who want to get off the street can find out about the help available. The next stage, for them, is permanent accommodation, but it's hard to organise that when you're living on a minimum youth allowance.'

Mike shook his head. His meal looked delicious but he knew he wouldn't taste it, his mind too full of what Jacinta had forced him to consider to recognise messages from his palate.

'So what's the answer?'

'Working together,' she said promptly. 'The government, the churches and other various charities do what they can, but until recently the whole system lacked cohesion. Some shelters didn't know others existed, and most of the kids had no idea of the range of options available to them.'

Talking hadn't put Jacinta off her food. She was eating her penne—with the smoked salmon sauce—with obvious enjoyment. Mike ate a little of his seafood lasagne, then had to ask.

'So what happened recently?'

She shot him a look he'd already seen—guilt and doubt combined with a small spark of hope. Then she smiled as if that might make everything OK.

Which it very nearly did.

'We started a thing called, for want of something smart or clever, "Optional Extras". I worked through government funding agencies and charities to contact all the youth services in and around the city, while Will and Dean scouted through the street kids for those they knew wanted to get their lives together.'

She paused but this time the smile was far more doubtful.

'We actually had the first meeting at the clinic—after hours, of course.'

Luminous brown eyes were fastened on his face, pleading with him to understand, so he knew darned well what was coming.

'We still meet there,' she admitted, and paused, waiting for a reaction.

Mike said nothing, wondering just what else might be going on at Abbott Road, then was distracted by the way the colour of her eyes almost exactly matched the colour of her hair.

'I tried to contact you to get permission but, as I think I explained last night, it's probably easier to speak to the Queen of England than to get through to you.'

The eyes were no longer pleading. In fact, they were daring him to tell her she'd done wrong.

But she already knew that.

'The clinic managers are in charge of the physical space at the clinic. You could have asked—' he knew this one, after all he only had six clinic managers, '—Carmel.'

Jacinta gave a long-suffering sigh and rolled her eyes, then returned to her penne with renewed gusto.

'She has the authority to allow such meetings,' Mike said, on firmer ground now as he'd personally been involved in drawing up the duty statements for different staff positions.

Still no answer. Jacinta was ignoring him, fishing through her side salad, presumably in search of something. An olive apparently, for, having found it, she speared it with her fork and raised it towards her lips.

'As if!' she muttered, then the olive disappeared, though the pip was discreetly removed by her small, slim fingers and dropped onto the side of the salad plate.

Mike was stymied. He knew he couldn't discuss one staff member with another. He might not have his finger on all the pulse points of his multi-tentacled empire, but he did retain some common decency. He ate a little more lasagne.

'So, what does the coming together of all the disparate groups achieve? What can your "Optional Extras" offer?'

'Information mainly,' Jacinta replied so smoothly he realised she'd been asked the question more than once. 'Information about the various sources of support and funding available—for both the services and for the kids. Information on how to get help, how to ask for help, where to go to ask.'

She looked up and studied him for a moment, as if checking his reaction to what she was saying.

'It's all available, the information, but before ''Optional Extras'' there wasn't any one place where people could access it all.'

'So Abbott Road Clinic became the place?'

Again she turned those searching eyes on his, scanning his face.

'Not during office hours,' she assured him. 'On Tuesdays we have ''Talk Nights'' when anyone can come and ask questions, or get help to fill out forms.'

'So once a week my premises are being used for illegal purposes?'

He saw the colour bleach from her skin and regretted his remark, but Jacinta didn't want his sympathy—she came back fighting.

'Hardly illegal!' she snapped. 'You make it sound like a brothel or a gambling den! And it's not doing the clinic any harm—in fact, since we started meeting there we've collected a number of new patients.'

All street kids, no doubt, Mike thought but didn't say.

As far as her employment contract was concerned, she'd been doing the wrong thing—and she knew it! But how to deal with it? He needed to think about it, and as his brain didn't seem to be thinking too well right now, he changed the subject.

'What are you doing about Fizzy? Did you ask the obstetrician to do a DNA profile on the foetus?'

Jacinta pushed away her plate and slid off her stool.

'Fizzy! I'm sitting here talking and she's probably thinking I've deserted her. They've such fragile egos, these kids. It doesn't take much to plunge them into despair.'

She fished in her handbag for her purse, but Mike caught hold of her wrist.

'I'm paying, and you didn't answer my question.'

Jacinta looked down at his hand, at the lean fingers effortlessly encircling her wrist. Tingles were happening again, but even more disconcerting was her recollection of his question.

'DNA profile? No, I didn't ask, but I still can. I asked the obstetrician to take foetal blood to test for abnormalities, though he'd have done it anyway. Normal procedure with such a late miscarriage, in case there's some genetic problem Fizzy should know about later in her life.'

She hesitated, then added, 'But DNA?'

'It would prove who had fathered the child.'

'But her stepfather…' The meaning of his words washed across her like a wave of cold water. 'You don't believe her story?'

She saw his doubts in the subtle movement of his shoulders and felt anger at his cynicism, but before she could argue he stood up, signalled to Marco for the bill, then said quietly, 'Whether I believe it or not isn't the point. At some time she may need proof her stepfather abused her, and having a DNA profile of the baby is the first and most necessary step.'

He was right, though Jacinta was still too aggravated by his attitude—and by the fact she hadn't thought of it—to admit it. *She* was the one who should have been thinking rationally. She had to set aside emotion. It was the only way to tackle the problems of these kids.

And definitely the only way to tackle the attraction she felt to Michael—Mike—Trent.

'I'll ask the obstetrician,' she said, halfway to admitting he was right.

He smiled, as if he knew exactly what she was thinking, and she lost the rational plot immediately, reacting to the smile with emotion—if tingling stomachs and goose-bumped skin could be called emotional reactions.

'Come on. We'd better get back to the clinic. You have to collect your car and I have some paintings to hang.'

He signed the credit-card slip Marco had produced, then took Jacinta's arm.

Thinking rationally, she accepted his hand on her elbow for as long as it took to be polite, then she moved away, out of the ambit of his body space—out of harm's way—or nearly!

The boys had gone and Fizzy was asleep when Jacinta returned to the hospital. The sister on night duty was warm and friendly, and had obviously pried most of Fizzy's story from her.

'Don't worry,' she told Jacinta as they stood by the nurses' station. 'I'll keep a close watch on her overnight, and if she wakes I'll tell her you came in. She'll probably be discharged in the morning. Is there somewhere she can go? Someone who might pick her up?'

'She can come to my place—my mother will collect her. I'll call in and see her in the morning. I'm due at work at seven-thirty and she won't be discharged before then.'

The sister nodded, and returned to whatever she'd been doing when Jacinta had arrived. As she walked out of the hospital memories of their arrival earlier, with Mike recurred and an image of him, bare-chested and paint-splattered, popped into Jacinta's head.

Get out of there! she told him, not wanting to think about the man—or the way her body behaved in his presence. She'd think about Fizzy and the other kids. About the new beginnings she'd helped put in place for all the youngsters who haunted the city like small, displaced ghosts.

Though she might have to think about what Mike would do next. Would he, even after meeting Fizzy, Will and Dean, forbid her to use the clinic for 'Optional Extras' meetings?

Would he sack her?

Now, there was a thought worth considering! If anything was going to cure her physical reactions to the head of Trent Clinics, the prospect of unemployment would surely work.

And would have if she hadn't started to wonder if he'd do it in person—so she'd have the opportunity to see him again.

*   *   *

The opportunity came sooner than Jacinta had expected. Even after visiting Fizzy and squashing the teenager's doubts about accepting help, Jacinta still arrived at work in plenty of time for Carmel's regular Monday morning medical staff meeting. And found her usual parking space taken up by a large, dark green Jaguar.

'Wow!'

Mark Sargeant, who job-shared with an older doctor while studying for a further degree, was standing by the car, admiring its lines, polish and, no doubt, price.

Jacinta parked beside it, taking the place usually occupied by the vehicle of Rohan Singh, the third GP in the clinic. Another space was reserved for Carmel, but if Rohan arrived first he'd take it without a moment's hesitation. Rohan had a sublime belief that whatever he did was right, and he'd somehow conned Carmel into believing it as well. She might nag at Jacinta and Mark about what she saw as infractions of the clinic rules, but in her eyes Rohan could do no wrong.

Jacinta and Mark walked towards the rear door, unlocked it and realised they weren't the first people here. There were lights on in the hall and the alarm had been disarmed.

'If it was Carmel's car, she'd have parked it in her own space,' Mark mused. 'Rohan, too, for that matter.'

But an uneasy feeling, not quite a tingle but close, in the pit of Jacinta's stomach told her whose car it might be.

There was no sign of him—only of Carmel, fussing at papers behind the high reception counter.

'She must have ridden her broomstick in this morning,' Mark murmured to Jacinta. 'For heaven's sake, don't trip over it if she's parked it somewhere awkward.'

'Is that all you're going to say?' Jacinta demanded. 'Look at this place!'

She waved her arms around, indicating the refurbished waiting room.

Mark glanced around as if noticing the change for the first time.

'Yeah! It looks nice. Bright! Actually, to be honest, I can't remember what it looked like before.'

Jacinta shook her head in disbelief. She knew all about men's and women's brains being wired differently, but she found it hard to comprehend anyone not noticing how terrible the waiting room had been.

'Come on, you two, I want to get started early,' Carmel called to them, then she waved them into the reception office.

He was sitting in a chair behind the high counter, which was why Jacinta hadn't noticed him until she was well into the room. And though dressed respectably, and totally paint-free, she was still put out enough to trip over the leg of one of the desks and practically stumble into his arms.

'I believe you've met Dr Trent, Jacinta,' Carmel said in a cool voice, while Jacinta attempted to recover both her balance and her breath. 'Dr Trent, this is Mark Sargeant, our third doctor. Mark, Dr Michael Trent.'

Jacinta watched Mike put out his hand to Mark, and heard the deep, seductive voice say, 'It's Mike, not Dr Trent, though I don't seem able to convince Carmel of that.'

Carmel gave a little laugh which, if Jacinta hadn't known better, could have sounded flustered. But flustered wasn't in Carmel's repertoire of emotions.

Was it?

'So, how's our young friend Fizzy this morning?'

Jacinta registered that Mike's question had been directed at her, but her mind was still getting over his presence in the clinic. Actually, other bits of her were getting over it as well.

'Fizzy? That's the pregnant girl? Fiona Walsh? What happened to her?'

Carmel's questions saved Jacinta answering, but Mike's explanations caused more problems.

'You had those unemployed layabouts in the clinic after hours?' Carmel demanded, and Jacinta, only too aware of the thin ice on which she'd been skating, had to grit her teeth really tightly to prevent an argument with the clinic manager.

'Should we get on with the meeting?' Mark saved the day.

'Rohan should be here any minute but while we're waiting for him, I'd like to congratulate Jacinta on the fine job she's done with the waiting room.'

He turned to beam at Jacinta, as if he he'd known all along she'd transformed the place. 'Love the paintings especially. Did you bring them from home?'

Mike saw through Mark's diversionary tactics and wondered if the young male doctor was in love with his colleague.

Wondered also how Jacinta would answer the question.

She didn't. She simply smiled her thanks at Mark, before turning to Carmel. 'It's not like Rohan to be late. Is he coming or has he phoned in sick?'

'Rohan's working at one of the other clinics this week,' Carmel replied. The words had a bitten-off sound to them as if she didn't approve of this change in personnel. 'Dr Trent will be working here in his place.'

Mike had seen patients take bad news more calmly than Jacinta accepted the last statement.

Colour flowed into her cheeks, then ebbed back out, leaving her face pale but her fighting spirit undaunted.

'But he can't. He hasn't practised for years!'

'I'm still registered,' Mike assured her, though he wondered why she was *so* upset. 'And I've kept up my professional training, making sure I attend the requisite number of seminars and information sessions, as well as keeping abreast of recent developments through journals.'

'I hardly think you're in a position to question Dr Trent's capabilities,' Carmel put in, and Mike saw Jacinta's soft lips close on the new objection she'd been about to voice.

But suspicion sparked from the dark eyes and the small, neat chin took on a stubborn tilt. As far as Jacinta was concerned, he was in for an uncomfortable time.

'I thought you wanted me to see Abbott Road for myself,' he murmured to her when the meeting had finished and they were walking across to their consulting rooms. 'What better way than by working here?'

'After how many years of not practising?' came the scathing

question. 'Is that offering the best possible service for patients?'

Confusion, brought on by her attitude, triggered anger. He'd already had his business manager, his accountant and Chris, his best mate as well as an employee, telling him he was mad, so he didn't need this pipsqueak of a woman adding her two cents' worth.

He glowered at her, then tried a different tack, saying in silky smooth tones, 'Ah, but you'll be right next door, ready to offer support, advice and encouragement—just as you would to any temporary staff member, surely?'

Jacinta delivered what she hoped was a sufficiently fierce glare and stomped into her consulting room. Patients were already drifting in, queuing at the reception desk, the regulars commenting about the improved appearance of the waiting room.

Mike was right. She *had* wanted him to see the place for himself, and what better way than by working here? Maybe there was more to the man than the 'business tycoon' image suggested.

But working right next door to her? Just through the wall? His presence permeating the air throughout the clinic?

She breathed deeply, defying the tainted air, and told herself she could handle the situation. It was a physical thing, this attraction she felt for him, and there was no way she was going to give in to it.

No more tingles.

No more goose-bumps.

No more time wasted thinking about him—picturing his lips, his unusual eyes, imagining softness in those eyes as his lips...

A patient card sliding into the box outside her door brought her up short. The day had begun. As soon as she opened her door and lifted the card, Carmel's eagle eye would notice and her voice would announce the appropriate number and direct him or her to Jacinta's room.

Number twenty-seven was a harassed-looking woman with a small child in tow.

'It's Bobby. I went to drop him at the childcare centre on my way to work and they say he's got a cold and can't stay there because he'll pass it on to all the other kids. Yet he must have caught it there. No one else in the family has a cold.'

The unspoken problem, Jacinta knew, was that the mother couldn't go to work unless Bobby was miraculously cured of the runny nose and sneezing fits he appeared to be suffering.

She knelt in front of the little boy.

'Let's take a look at you. It's not much fun, having a cold, is it?'

She took his temperature, slightly raised, listened to his chest—clear considering the amount of fluids issuing from his nose—checked his throat—not infected—and sighed.

'It *is* just a cold,' Jacinta told his mother—Mrs Armitage, according to the card. 'But he is infectious and I can understand the childcare centre staff not wanting him sneezing all over other kids. And there's really not much you can do, apart from giving him plenty of fluids and a mild children's analgesic if he complains of a headache. Is there anyone else who can mind him? A relative perhaps?'

Mrs Armitage glanced at her watch.

'One of the older kids could have stayed home, but they'll have left for school by now.' She sighed. 'I guess it means me. I'll have to phone my boss and tell him, and who knows what he'll say? It's hard enough getting a job these days, but keeping one, when you've got kids as well...'

'Would you like to use my phone?' Jacinta suggested, knowing Carmel wouldn't offer. 'Save you dragging him up the mall to the public phone.'

She got an outside line, handed the receiver to Mrs Armitage, then knelt down to occupy Bobby while his mother made her call. She found a small truck in the box of toys she kept for children, and was buzzing it across the carpet when a knock sounded on the door.

'Come in,' she called, shooting the truck across to Bobby.

The door opened and Mike appeared, just as Bobby, not satisfied with running the truck on the floor, turned it into an airborne craft and flung it across the room.

Jacinta ducked and it banged harmlessly into the wall, but as she scrambled inelegantly to her feet she could feel the heat of new embarrassment stealing into her cheeks.

Fortunately, Mrs Armitage finished her call and bent to lift her son into her arms.

'Come on, little nuisance,' she said, though her voice was loving. 'Thanks, Doctor.'

Mike held the door as the pair departed.

'Thanks for nothing!' Jacinta muttered to herself, then she looked at Mike. 'What this city needs is a place where kids who aren't too well can be cared for while their parents work. I'm not talking about really ill children, just those with coughs and colds who aren't acceptable at their regular childcare centre.'

The puzzled expression on his face stopped her fretful comments.

'I'm sorry. I was thinking out loud. Did you want something?'

Mike considered a range of replies, the most surprising of which, he found, was a single word. You!

Ridiculous!

He couldn't possibly want Jacinta Ford.

Look at her! A small, neat woman with an admittedly shapely body, but packed with problems. There she was, frowning at the door, worrying about a woman she'd probably never met before and planning more good works. He'd met women like her, women who put the welfare of others before the comfort and well-being of their own families.

Though why he'd think of family with Jacinta…

'You can't solve the problems of the entire inner city,' he told her, but when the dark eyes turned his way, and the twin arcs of her eyebrows rose, he found himself adding, 'Well, not overnight.'

She smiled, conceding his point—and starting an argument in his head about why he shouldn't want her.

Because she's not your type, and she's been trouble from the word go, and—

'Can I help you?'

'No!'

The reply was automatic, given the way he was thinking, so he had to amend it.

'Actually, yes. Do we have a policy for patients who want prescriptions for strong pain relief?'

'The ones that say, "Doctor, I'm in agony from my back. It happened ages ago and a doctor gave me a tablet called something forte." That kind of thing?'

Jacinta had repeated almost word for word what Mike's first patient had said, then shrugged as if this was one problem she hadn't yet solved.

'We don't have a policy, but most GPs are aware there are addicted patients who go from doctor to doctor with the same story. I usually tell those patients it could be something worse, like severe kidney disease, which a high codeine concentration could exacerbate. Then I send them off for X-rays and suggest they might need an ultrasound as well. Usually they take the X-ray form but never have it done.'

'And what if they're genuinely in severe pain from a back problem?' Mike asked, secretly impressed by this very practical strategy.

'Then they'll be only too happy to have the X-ray, which they can do within an hour at the radiology clinic just up the road. They can bring the X-ray and the report back, then I see them straight away, and if there is a problem, I prescribe.'

She sighed.

'And I know I can still be conned. I know they can go to another doctor in a couple of days and do exactly the same thing and get more codeine to feed their habit. But at least I've seen an actual problem.'

Jacinta frowned at him.

'Have you someone waiting in your consulting room, while Bobby's been throwing trucks and I've been prattling on?'

Mike smiled at her concern.

'No. I actually thought of the X-ray thing for myself and sent him off, but I checked his file and saw he came in to see Rohan for prescriptions regularly.'

'Some patients do,' she said, and again he read her commitment to her work in the way she frowned as she said it, as if this was one more problem she'd like to solve. Though whether it was the doctor who prescribed the drugs or the possibly addicted patient she was frowning over, Mike couldn't guess.

She walked to the door and took up a new card from the box outside, and Mike heard Carmel call instructions to the next patient.

He took Jacinta's movement as dismissal, but as he returned to his temporary consulting room he was more confused than ever.

The number thing would have to go—that much was clear. It was downright impersonal.

And maybe he'd have to figure some way to check on the performance of the doctors in his practices. If someone was over-prescribing, would it show up somewhere in Trent Clinics' records, or would the firm only find out when a law suit hit them?

While as for Jacinta Ford…

He set that question aside—after all, what he felt for Jacinta was only a passing attraction. But getting back to basics as far as the clinics were concerned, maybe that was something he should have done some time ago.

He lifted the phone, got an outside line and phoned Chris. *He* could explain Mike's decision to the other executives because he'd be less shocked by it. Chris tried to spend a month doing hands-on work in one of the clinics each year, because, he said, he wanted to know the kind of workload the doctors he employed had to handle.

Though if he'd worked with someone as feisty as Jacinta, surely he'd have mentioned her…

CHAPTER SIX

'DO YOU examine all your patients?'

Jacinta looked up from the paperwork she was trying to finish before leaving clinic. It was Thursday and she was still trying to come to terms with having Mike working in the room alongside hers at the clinic.

And trying to hold at bay the attraction towards him that had flared within her body from the moment she'd first heard his voice.

'Of course I do. What kind of question is that?'

She dropped her pen, realising it made the trembling in her fingers more obvious.

Trembling caused by surprise, she told herself, not the man himself.

'Even if they're repeat patients you've seen before and who only require a script?'

She frowned at his persistence. He'd come into the room now and had propped himself across the desk from her, his hands on the back of one of her patient chairs.

'I have to, don't I? Otherwise I wouldn't know if whatever I've prescribed is doing any good.'

'So, if a patient comes in and asks for more of his cream, and you know he suffers from piles, you'd still examine him?'

'Piles can often be cured by a very simple day-surgery operation. I'd have suggested that before cream.'

She cocked her head to one side, reminding him of an inquisitive little bird.

'Are you asking for some reason? If not, I've a heap of work to do before I can get away, and as I've dumped Fizzy on my mother for the next few weeks, and the boys are visiting tonight, I really should get home some time this evening.'

Mike felt a nudge of disappointment in his chest and realised that subconsciously he must have been considering asking her to dinner. Something he'd also considered on Monday, Tuesday and Wednesday.

It had to stop.

He was about to explain the reason for his question when a loud banging on the clinic's front door stopped all further questions.

'Is someone still there? Please, be there! Open up, please?'

Jacinta reacted almost immediately, but Mike had been closer to the consulting-room door and was out first, disarming the alarm and opening the door without a second thought.

'There *is* a spy hole. You're supposed to check,' she murmured, as he grabbed the hysterical man by the shoulders and tried to calm him.

'No, it's not me, it's my father—he's collapsed. Up in the mall. Someone's called an ambulance, but I knew there was a clinic here. You have to help.'

'You go with him,' Jacinta said to Mike. 'I'll lock up and join you as soon as possible. If necessary three quick breaths then chest compression. I'll do the air as soon as I get there.'

Mike went with the young man, his own heart racing as he considered such a thing happening to his own father. The man lay only fifteen metres from the clinic entrance, surrounded by a crowd of onlookers, mostly shop and office staff heading home after a day's work.

Apart from the fact that someone had put a jacket over the man's legs, no one was doing anything.

Mike knelt beside him, felt for a pulse beneath his chin and, finding nothing, bent to clasp the man's nose, open his mouth, clear his airway, then blow three quick breaths into his lungs.

'OK, I'm here,' he heard Jacinta say. 'You know the drill—you're happy to do the compressions? You'd have more strength, you see.'

She knelt beside him and they worked in unison, Mike compressing the thick chest with enough strength to cause bruised ribs while Jacinta blew brain-saving oxygen into the man's lungs, stopping to let his body release the unwanted gases, then breathing life into him again.

But there was still no pulse when the ambulance arrived, and Jacinta quietly moved the crowd on so the ambulancemen could try electric shock to resuscitate him.

With the efficiency born of dealing with emergencies, the attendants nodded to Mike to keep up the compressions while they hooked the patient up to a monitor and prepared to use shock to restart his heart.

No response but they slid him onto a stretcher then tried again, and Mike knew they'd continue their efforts on the way to the hospital. But in his heart he knew they'd failed, and the thought of his own father losing his life in a similar situation filled him with a dark despair.

They waited until the ambulance had departed, then returned to the clinic. Jacinta, all senses on full alert whenever she was near Mike, was aware of a heaviness in the way he moved, as if the failure to revive the man was his alone.

'He may still live,' she said, but though Mike cast her a surprised look, he didn't respond. When she unlocked the door and they entered the still lit waiting room, he slumped into a chair and motioned her to take another one.

'Sit!'

It was an order, and while on other days she might have objected to the way he spoke—as part of her keeping her attraction to him at bay—tonight she sat.

And waited.

Mike frowned at her. He'd come to learn such immediate compliance wasn't in Jacinta's nature—come to learn a lot about the woman who'd embroiled him in this ridiculous 'back to his beginnings' idea. But tonight there was more on his mind than Jacinta Ford—for which, he decided, he should be thankful.

'There must have been twenty-five people all standing around that man for ten minutes or more while his son went for help. I thought CPR was widely taught these days. Damn it all, it isn't hard to do, and could have saved that man's life if someone had started it immediately.'

'It's taught in schools, but kids probably don't take a lot of notice, then they forget.' Jacinta looked doubtful. 'I think people can opt to learn it. Most hospitals run courses from time to time.'

'Which people won't attend because it's out of their way. What about this clinic? Couldn't we do it? Time them so people could attend in their lunch hours? Or after work? We could shift the chairs, get a couple of dummies, educate at least a percentage of inner city workers.'

He was thinking of whether the scheme could be effective in his other clinics, and how lessons could be incorporated into the internet site, when he realised his colleague hadn't responded to his suggestion.

He glanced her way and caught a smile hovering on her lips and laughter glinting in the dark eyes.

'And here was I thinking we couldn't solve the problems of the entire inner city,' she teased. 'Well, not overnight.'

There was something so unsettling about being teased by Jacinta that Mike bit back an answering smile.

'It would hardly solve the problems of the entire inner city,' he said, as coolly as his heated blood would allow. 'And now the drama's over, I'd better be off. Getting back to basics in medical practice doesn't mean the rest of my business has come to a standstill.'

It was a reminder to himself, as well as her, that he had responsibilities ranging way beyond this clinic. And he'd needed the reminder, because what he'd wanted to say had been, How about dinner? Even though he'd come to realise his employee's worth as a doctor and contributing member of his staff, he certainly didn't want to get involved with her.

From the way she'd spoken about relationships and her parents' marriage, she certainly wasn't the kind of woman you could take out for a while—one with whom you could perhaps enjoy a mutually satisfactory sexual relationship—then move on from without hesitation or guilt.

Particularly guilt.

Jacinta tried to remember what they'd been discussing before the young man had summoned them to help his father. Mike had asked a question, but she couldn't for the life of her remember what it had been. Her brain too concerned with convincing her that his show of concern and compassion for the stricken man didn't make any difference to the fact he wasn't for her, no matter how her body felt about him.

She looked at him, wondering about chemistry and why one man could have such a physical effect on her body when she saw and worked with men every day of her life without the slightest physical reaction to them. Then her mind went beyond personal problems because, though he'd said he had to be going, he was still sitting in the waiting room. Something in the stillness of his body and the lines of tiredness in his face reached out to touch her heart.

'Are you OK?'

He swung towards her, frowning now as if shocked by the question.

'Why shouldn't I be?' he snapped, and Jacinta straightened in her chair and told him.

'Because you look exhausted, and it's no wonder if you're working here all day then going back to your office and trying to do a full day's work there each night. Surely you've got executives who can handle most of that. You really don't need to be here. I wanted you to see the place, not kill yourself trying to do two jobs at once.'

'Trying to get rid of me, Jacinta?' The slight smile accompanying the words made her realise that was exactly what she should be doing, but she stuck to her guns.

'No, I'm not. I'm just being sensible. You can't go on like this—and it's not necessary anyway. You've seen the place—you must realise what's needed. That's all I wanted.'

Mike's smile faded.

'Is it?' he said softly, and when she didn't answer, he sighed and shook his head.

'Anyway, I won't be here tomorrow,' he said, rising to his

feet. I've a business trip I can't put off, but I get back Monday. Having said I'd do a week, I'll do a week. So I'll see you Tuesday.'

He stopped, as if waiting for a reaction from her, and though Jacinta's heart had plummeted at the 'won't be here tomorrow' scenario and had then gone into a dance of delight at 'I'll see you Tuesday', she didn't think she'd share either of these reactions with him.

So she nodded, as if it were of no consequence whatever when he came and went.

'And I've remembered what it was we were discussing. I've learnt how busy you are during the day, so perhaps we could have dinner Tuesday evening and talk it over then.'

'Dinner? Tuesday evening? With you?'

Obviously she was as startled by the question as Mike had been when he'd heard himself asking it, but did she have to sound quite so incredulous?

'A purely business arrangement—convenient really,' he said, hopefully projecting cool, professional control. 'And you *have* eaten with me before. I didn't bite or display revolting table manners, did I?'

'But Tuesday? There's a meeting here.'

The lack of regret—or any kind of emotion—in her voice made him persist.

'Great!' He could do hearty as well as the next man, when the need arose. 'I'd like to sit in on the meeting, see what goes on, then we can eat afterwards. If I remember rightly, Marco's stays open later on weeknights.'

Sure he'd sewn her up this time, he smiled, nodded his head, then said, 'See you Tuesday.' And whisked out the door before she could find another objection.

Jacinta saw the door close behind him but, like the Cheshire cat in *Alice*, his smile seemed to remain.

She knew it was as natural to him as breathing—flashing that charming grin—but knowing he did it so easily didn't affect its potency in any way. Only this time it was her toes tingling while her stomach was twisting into the kind of knot she doubted common sense would unravel.

Anyway, there was one consolation. On Tuesdays she always bought pizza for everyone and they ate during the meeting, so there'd be no need to go out to dinner afterwards.

Work seemed dull and flat on Friday and Monday, so by Tuesday Jacinta wasn't certain whether to be glad or sorry the day had finally arrived. She'd slept badly, haunted by dreams of a man with black, silver-flecked hair, a handsomely craggy face and changeable eyes. He'd been holding her in his arms, tucking her tightly against his body, his kisses arousing feelings she'd only dreamed of—but she *had* been dreaming. Again and again she'd forced herself awake, only to slide back into the same scenario, but always at the beginning so she never learnt the end...

And though she tried to tell herself the attraction was purely physical, she knew from seeing Mike at work the previous week—seeing him with patients, with the man who'd had the heart attack—there was more to Mike Trent than her research had led her to believe. So it was hard not to be impressed by the man she'd begun to know.

She dressed for work, reluctant for once to leave the security of her home yet choosing what to wear as carefully as if the dinner after the meeting was to be a real date.

Mike, early for reasons he didn't want to consider, saw her walk in. She was wearing a slim-fitting, creamy-coloured dress that buttoned down the front with the buttons from knee to the hem at mid-calf undone, so he caught flashes of suntanned legs as she strode purposefully into the waiting room.

'Morning, all,' she said, her eyes carefully avoiding Mike's as she nodded her greeting to the staff—himself, Carmel and one office worker. The fact that she showed absolutely no interest in him as a man was both irritating, given how she affected him, and intriguing—could she be so totally unaffected by an attraction so strong he found it hard to believe it could be one-sided?

He manoeuvred himself into a position where she'd have to pass close by him as she went to her consulting room, and pretended to read her bulletin board.

'Meeting tonight?' he murmured, as she drew close.

She flashed a glance towards Carmel, which told him the clinic manager had no idea of this particular doctor's extra-curricular activities.

'It could go late,' she said, and he guessed she was trying to squirm out of the dinner arrangement.

'Oh, I rarely eat early,' Mike said, enjoying the colour creeping into her cheeks and delighting in the way she lifted her eyes to study his face, as if trying to read exactly what was going on in his mind.

Just as well she couldn't.

'We don't *have* to go to dinner, you know. We could discuss whatever it is you want to discuss right here.'

'Running scared, Jacinta?' he teased, and more delicious colour washed into her cheeks.

'Why should I be?' she demanded, tilting her chin towards him but unable to hide an uncertainty in her velvety brown eyes.

He leaned towards her, but before he had time to take the subject further raucous voices on the stairs alerted all the staff to the possibility of an all-hands-on-deck crisis.

Three men erupted into the waiting room, pushing the door open so violently that Carmel, who'd gone across to unlock it while Mike spoke to Jacinta, was flung to the ground.

'Get them off me, stop them, keep them away from me!'

The central figure in the group danced madly around the room, flinging his arms around his head and flapping his hands as if to ward off a swarm of bees.

'Get them away! Stop them! For…'

The language deteriorated and Mike stepped in front of Jacinta who'd tried to hurry, oblivious to the potential danger, towards the man.

'What's happened?' he asked one of the two companions.

'Something he took. He hasn't injected but we don't know

what else he had. He was OK at breakfast then we took a walk downtown and suddenly this. He says they're flying piranhas, trying to eat his flesh.'

Mike had grabbed the man as his friend explained, but he was effortlessly flung backward by the manic strength of the hallucinating addict. Then the two friends caught the man and somehow got him to a chair while Mike turned to Jacinta, who'd helped Carmel up and seen her safely back to the security of the office.

'What do we keep that might calm him?'

'Hallucinations are most common with narcotics, opiates, morphine, derivatives or synthetic agonist compounds. Naloxone hydrochloride—we keep that in the drug safe in the office—would work as an antidote on any of those, but if it's not a narcotic—'

'What harm could it do?'

Jacinta tried to think—were there contra-indications? Long term, yes, but as a quick fix until they got the man to hospital?

'None,' she said, 'but giving it to him is going to be the problem.'

Mike watched as the man, who'd escaped the custody of his mates, climbed onto one of the newly covered chairs and went capering up and down the room, stepping from one to the next, balancing so precariously he could fall at any minute.

'Get it ready and I'll try,' he told Jacinta. 'Mark's here now. With him and the two friends, we should be able to manage.'

She hurried across to the office where Carmel had already opened the drug safe.

'I've phoned for the ambulance. They're on their way, but with peak-hour traffic it could take a while.'

Jacinta paused to thank her, then found all she needed. She took a swab, the filled syringe and gloves across to Mark, who was talking quietly to the traumatised man, trying to convince him that a quick jab of a needle would get rid of the voracious fish.

As Jacinta approached, Mike put out his arm, slowly and

carefully so he didn't startle the patient, and tucked Jacinta behind him.

'I can look after myself!' she hissed at his broad back, but he ignored her, continuing to talk to the man until he quietened and eventually stepped down off the chair and slumped into it instead.

Mike seized the moment—and the syringe—thrusting the sharp point of the needle into the man's skin, injecting the fluid and withdrawing it, almost before the confused individual had time to realise what was happening.

'You didn't put on gloves,' Jacinta muttered at Mike. 'That's a stupid risk to take.'

'Would you have?' Mike demanded, ushering her away from the man while his friends again took over as custodians. 'And missed that fraction of a second when you could safely inject?'

Jacinta knew she wouldn't have, but wasn't going to admit it. Any more than she was going to admit how well Mike had handled the situation. Or that the more she saw of him, the more impressed she was.

With his doctoring, that was.

She stomped off to her consulting room, furious with herself that she was letting a man—any man—so dominate her thoughts.

Not any more! she promised herself. Not for one second longer.

Patients would soon be arriving, and she had test results to check and file, letters to write to specialists, a dozen little tasks to do. All of which were more important than thinking about Mike Trent and the confusion he was causing in her body, mind and spirit.

'Well, that wasn't too bad, was it?'

The same Mike Trent Jacinta had spent all day trying to ignore apparently thought a day when only one addict ran amok in the waiting room was reason for celebration. He and Mark were leaning on the reception counter, chatting to the office girls and the clinic nurses, who were slumped in chairs and sipping at glasses of wine, provided in honour of one of their birthdays. Carmel wasn't slumped, neither was she sipping wine, but she was there—and smiling sycophantically at Mike.

Jacinta walked past the two men and into the reception area, returning files to the long shelves of patient records, discreetly hidden from public view by a false wall at the back of the reception area.

'We don't get many problems like that fellow, though we seem to be seeing an increasing number of addicts,' Mark said. 'No doubt due to Jacinta's good works.'

'We've really no way of weeding them out,' Carmel complained. 'It's one of the reasons I think the clinic should close.'

Jacinta paused in her task and held her breath. They'd all seen her walk in so it wasn't as if she was eavesdropping, but she was too tired to get into an argument over the clinic right now.

'I know when you set it up, Mike,' Carmel continued— she'd finally dropped the Dr Trent—'you intended the service for workers in the city who couldn't access medical services after hours, but now that your suburban clinics are open both early and late, most people can get to a doctor either before or after work. So we're losing those decent kinds of patients and all we're gaining in their place are the no-hopers.'

'We still see a fair number of city office and shop workers,' Mark protested, but it was a half-hearted effort. Knowing the job was only a stop-gap for him, Jacinta understood his lack of commitment.

She shoved the last of the files away, and came out from behind the wall.

Mike must have been waiting for her to reappear, for he cocked one eyebrow at her and allowed a small flicker of a smile to play about his lips as he said, 'Any comment?'

'Why should there be?' she snapped at him, but before she could say more, Carmel was complaining about her presence near the filing shelves.

'You know the girls do all the filing, Jacinta. You doctors don't seem to understand the system—you put the files just anywhere.'

Jacinta thought about telling her that as she wasn't colour blind, could count and knew her alphabet, she was just as capable as 'the girls' to handle filing, but she knew her anger had been caused by the closing-the-clinic comment, not the filing remark, so she merely nodded and escaped back to her consulting room.

She had another worry to consume her now. Although the staff usually celebrated each other's birthdays with a quick drink after work, they were always gone by seven-thirty when the 'Optional Extras' meetings got under way. But tonight she had an uneasy feeling Carmel would stay as long as Mike was here, so she'd find out about the meetings and add another black mark to Jacinta's record.

Though, with Mike here, tacitly giving consent...

Shame that she could even think of using him as protective colouring was only fleeting. No! If Mike Trent approved the use of the clinic, Carmel could hardly object. Perhaps having dinner with him wasn't such a bad idea. It would give her the opportunity to get formal permission for the meetings to continue.

She sighed and rested her chin on her hands, staring blankly at the door that hid the man from view. Committed though she was to the survival of the clinic, she also knew, deep down, that she was making excuses to spend time with him.

'You're mad!' she muttered to herself. 'He's so far out of your league you might as well exist on different planets. And as he's not for you, why exacerbate what's already a very inconvenient attraction, by spending time alone with him?'

And though she asked herself the question out loud, it was a tiny inner voice that answered.

Because you want to know how the dream ended?

'Balderdash!'

She used the word, gleaned from her fascination with Regency novels, forcefully, but it lacked its usual punch. Was there something else that would convince her wayward body that dining with Mike Trent was like playing on the rim of an active volcano?

Bloody hell?

She tried it out loud as Mike walked into the room.

'Am I so unwelcome?' he asked, and she knew from the twinkle in his eyes that he was laughing at her.

'No,' she grumbled, then recognised the dishonesty of her reply. 'Yes, actually, you are. You're messing up my life.'

'*I'm* messing up *your* life?'

In other circumstances, his incredulity might have been funny—but not today.

'Yes, you are,' she snapped at him, then found she couldn't go on. Which was just as well for he wouldn't have taken any notice. He had already launched into his own complaint.

'Do you think I want to be down here, wrestling with drug addicts, while my senior staff email me every second of the day, demanding to know when I'll be back? It's all very well for you to say I should see for myself, but a business this size doesn't run itself, you know. Someone has to be at the helm, making decisions, forward planning, spreading the financial risk—'

'Considering the money, not the people!'

Aware there were staff still in the clinic, Jacinta had left her chair to walk around behind him and shut the door, and now she'd paused, not a foot from him, to deliver her dart.

He grabbed her by the shoulders.

'One of the people is getting a darned sight too much consideration,' he growled, then the lips she'd fantasised about came down on hers in precisely the way they had in the dream, and he tucked her close to his long, hard body, just as he had in the dream, and—

Someone knocked on the door?

That hadn't happened in the dream, though it had usually stopped just as abruptly.

'I'm leaving now, Mike.' Carmel's honeyed words carried

clearly through the door. 'You're sure I can't get you anything before I go?'

'You have to open it and talk to her,' Jacinta muttered at him, peeling herself from his body and trying to still the trembling in her knees.

But as he turned to the door and opened it, her gaze followed him, riveted to him as she tried to work out why he'd kissed her—and whether it had had as tumultuous an effect on him as it had on her.

The low murmur of his voice and Carmel's trilling laugh came through to her, but nothing made any sense any more, so Jacinta was still standing, as if she'd taken root on the spot, when he shut the door and turned to face her.

'I suppose if I kiss you again someone else will interrupt. What time do all your lame ducks start arriving?'

If he kisses me again, I'll probably faint—that was Jacinta's first thought, but she pulled herself together sufficiently to protest at his derogatory remark.

'Most of the members of "Optional Extras" are service providers or their staff, or government employees working in youth-related fields. They are *not* lame ducks.'

'But they'll probably arrive, won't they?' Mike persisted, as if he really wanted to kiss her again.

Jacinta forced herself to think of the elegant blonde who'd called him 'darling' on Saturday night.

'I don't see that it matters,' she said crossly. 'Any more than I can understand why you'd even want to kiss a little brown mouse like me when you've got that very kissable blonde at your disposal. I'm not here for your amusement, you know.'

Mike shook his head and looked gravely down at her.

'If there's anything even vaguely amusing in this situation, I have yet to find it,' he grumbled. 'And, believe me, this kissing thing is just as puzzling to me as it must be to you. As you said, there's Jaclyn...'

His voice trailed away and he edged closer, and though Jacinta knew exactly what was about to happen—after all, she'd dreamed it just this way—she didn't move, except to tilt her chin so when Mike's lips claimed hers, she was ready. She slipped her hands around his shoulders and clung on for support, kissing him as thoroughly as he was kissing her—taking herself into uncharted territory, way beyond the boundaries of the dream.

Of any dream!

'Jacinta, your pizzas are here.'

This time Mark's voice interrupted, and she broke away from Mike, grabbed her handbag from the bottom drawer of her desk and was about to rush out the door when Mike's hand grasped her shoulder.

'We *are* having dinner together later?' he said, his voice so husky she could feel it stroke across her skin.

Too confused to speak, she nodded, then, as she fled out the door, regretted the movement. Having dinner with him was equivalent to abandoning the rim of the volcano by leaping into the inferno.

Not a good idea.

Mike watched her pay a pizza delivery youth, then deposit the boxes on a table at the back of the waiting room. Mark was pulling chairs into a circle. Did he stay on because he was as committed to the street kids as Jacinta was, or because he fancied her?

He only worked part time—maybe he liked the free feed!

What Mark did or didn't do was none of his business, Mike reminded himself, but that didn't stop him scowling at the younger man, who'd just patted Jacinta on her neat little backside.

Fortunately, people began arriving, greeting Jacinta and Mark, grabbing a slice of pizza before settling down on chairs. Mike was surprised to see quite senior government employees taking their places beside kids like Dean and Will. A vaguely familiar older woman—maybe Jacinta's mother—had come in with Will and Dean, and Mike, from his vantage point near the consulting-room door, studied her.

'You can join us if you wish.'

Jacinta's clear voice rose above the buzz of conversation, and Mike, who'd been considering how attractive Jacinta would still be in middle age, was startled into movement.

'Everyone,' Jacinta continued, 'the gentleman up the back is Dr Mike Trent, head of Trent Clinics, here to see what nefarious plots we're hatching in his waiting room.'

General laughter greeted this remark, and a couple of men and women he knew from government committee work turned to greet him. Then everyone settled down, Jacinta called the meeting to order and discussion began.

'I can't believe we've achieved so much in such a short time,' the woman sitting beside Mike whispered, while one speaker was sorting through his notes for some figures he'd apparently lost. 'Only a couple of months ago we were all doing our own thing. It was like applying Band-Aids to a burst blood vessel. I'm Bonnie Curtis, by the way. I run Teen Scene.'

'The group that's setting up the new permanent accommodation house? I've seen it on television and read of it in the papers.'

'That's it,' Bonnie said cheerfully. 'It'll be up and running in a couple of weeks, with young Fizzy, Will, Dean, a girl named Charis and a youngster called Jarrod—he's at night school tonight—moving in as the first boarders. Looking around here at the paint job Jacinta did over the weekend, I feel a bit guilty. She's the one who got the ''Kids Helping Kids'' group going, and I had them all helping me paint on Sunday.'

The 'Kids Helping Kids' remark rang no bells, so Mike was about to ask about funding for the house where the young people would live when the speaker found his notes and started explaining the figures.

These more or less answered the question Mike hadn't asked. A group that raised money to be spent specifically on projects for young people had paid for the house. The government would subsidise the wages of two house-parents, and the 'boarders' would all pay a portion of their youth allowance towards their board and keep.

Discussions on security of the premises followed, then the talk moved on to shelters and the need for them to be more adaptable to the needs of the young people who used them.

'I hadn't realised there were so many interconnected problems,' he whispered to Bonnie, as a young woman expressed a concern about the hours shelters could open.

'Been living too long in the fleshpots of Forest Glen?' she murmured.

He smiled at her.

'I'm certainly out of touch,' he admitted, though he did wonder how everyone in the world seemed to know about his life and lifestyle while he knew so little about what was happening back here where it had all begun.

He was still considering this conundrum when the meeting finished. Mark collected the empty pizza boxes and took them out to the rubbish. Mike decided Carmel *must* know about the meetings as the smell of pizza wouldn't disappear overnight, but before he had time to follow up this thought Jacinta came towards him and he shifted his attention to her.

So it was disconcerting when she walked straight past him to give the woman he'd noticed with the boys a quick kiss.

There was a murmured conversation, too low for Mike to catch, but if he thought his 'date' was going to introduce him to her relative, he was doomed to disappointment. Mrs Ford was already heading for the stairs with Will and Dean—who'd earlier come over to shake his hand—walking on either side of her.

'I guessed that was your mother. What does she do in all this?' he asked, when Jacinta appeared by his side.

'Care?' she said, a teasing glint in her eye.

'Actually,' she relented, 'she's one of those much-maligned creatures, a social worker. She only works part time these days. But she *does* care, and she's also very knowledgeable about long-term consequences of decisions I tend to take without thinking.'

Mike wanted to ask for a 'for instance', but he also wanted to kiss her again. As that didn't seem a very good idea, he suggested they depart. 'After all, I've been here since seven-thirty this morning, which makes it a fourteen-hour day—longer than I can afford to pay me.'

Jacinta chuckled, but he sensed relief in the way she hurried off to get her handbag and lock her consulting room.

They left by the front door, again walking through the mall. His toe was better now so there was no excuse to hold her hand.

Would she mind if he did anyway?

Feeling as uncertain as a teenager on his first date, Mike strode briskly along the familiar route.

'Ghosts chasing you?' Jacinta asked, bringing his steps to an abrupt halt. 'Not that I mind walking quickly. It was the running to keep up I found hard.'

He looked down into her flushed face and saw doubt as well as amusement in the dark depths of her lovely eyes.

'Sorry. I tend to stride out a bit when I'm thinking.'

They walked on, though he'd shortened his steps and lessened his pace.

'Thinking of closing down Abbott Road, or of stopping it being used as a meeting place?'

Mike knew frown lines, which at his age he couldn't afford to encourage, had gathered on his forehead. Weren't women supposed to be the sentimental gender—ruled by emotion rather than rational thought? Yet, while he was thinking of dates, and hand-holding and the possibility of kissing her again in the not too distant future, his companion's only concern was work-related.

The problem was, he *should* be thinking of closing down Abbott Road. According to a late email from his accountant, he would have to sell the building to fund the planned expansion and the internet venture. Though now was hardly the time to tell Jacinta.

Actually, now was precisely the time to tell Jacinta, his

conscience growled, but before he could mentally debate the issue she spoke again.

'I'm sorry. I shouldn't have brought it up. Of course, you'll do whatever's right for you, but there are alternatives to closing down, you know. Restructuring would make it more profitable. Abbott Road doesn't need the number of—'

Mike stopped moving, turned towards her and rested his hands on her shoulders.

'Do you think we could, just for a couple of hours, forget about Abbott Road? I promise I'll listen to your ideas tomorrow. We'll make a time and sit down and talk about nothing else.'

Jacinta looked up into his face, and in the light from a nearby lamp he could see bewilderment written on her face, doubt flickering in her eyes.

'But if we're not having dinner to discuss business,' she said, her voice small and slightly wavery, 'why are we having it?'

Why indeed? asked the cynic in his head.

'Could we pretend it's just a…?' He hesitated. To use the word 'date' might put her off altogether. 'Social occasion?'

He could all but see the word 'why' hovering on her lips, but he turned away, tucked her hand into the crook of his arm and moved on, thinking of the silly, sentimental phrase 'as high as my heart'.

To have silly sentimental phrases or thoughts bumbling about in his head raised red flags of warning. Treacherous path ahead.

'That's a ridiculous suggestion!' his companion said, after an interval so long he thought he'd convinced her. 'Apart from both being doctors, we've nothing in common and, if you remember, you all but blackmailed me into coming out with you tonight by suggesting we discuss the clinic.'

His mind flashed back to when he *had* asked her out and he remembered they hadn't been discussing the survival of the clinic but prescription drugs.

'OK, so we'll talk, but not until we've had a drink, relaxed and at least started on our meal. For now, let's enjoy the stroll. I love the city when it's emptying of people. A cloak of mystery seems to wrap around it—as if there's no knowing what might be going on behind the closed shop and office doors.'

'Toys coming to life and dancing around the toyshops?' Jacinta teased, though she knew she shouldn't give in to the light-hearted mood enveloping her. Surely the kissing thing that afternoon was enough to remind her to keep their relationship on a business footing.

But, no, here she was, her hand tucked cosily into Mike's elbow, her body moving by his side, in step with his—and being light-hearted!

'I was thinking more in terms of secret meetings,' he countered, and she heard amusement in his voice. 'Assignations!'

'Assignations!' she repeated, ignoring the dig about the secret meetings. 'It has such an illicit sound. Like stolen kisses.'

Now, what had made her add that? Mentioning kisses had prompted her heart to skitter about with a dangerous delight. Not exactly a good start to the 'business footing'.

'Stolen kisses?' His turn to repeat a snippet of conversation. 'Is that what we shared, Jacinta?'

They'd reached the restaurant and he paused outside it, turning so he could look down into her face.

She met his gaze without flinching and said, with a forthrightness she was far from feeling, 'What else could they be, Mike? We're chalk and cheese, you and I, and even if we did have something in common, you don't want commitment while I, if I'm going to invest my time and energy in a relationship, would definitely want to think it had some hope of lasting. I'm beyond the let's-just-have-fun stage in my life.'

He looked slightly put out, then his eyes sparked with what she was beginning to recognise as a smile, and she knew he'd decided to turn it into a joke.

'So we can't just have some fun?'

For a brief moment Jacinta was tempted. In fact, part of her was arguing it was time she had a little fun. Then, attracted though she might be to the man, she remembered the volcano.

If kissing him caused such reactions, 'having fun' with Mike Trent, a man who wanted nothing to do with long-term attachments, would undoubtedly consume her, leaving nothing but the charred ruins of the Jacinta she'd once been.

'No!'

CHAPTER SEVEN

MIKE watched Jacinta slide into one side of the booth. She looked—and had sounded—so composed and cool that if he hadn't tasted her kisses and heard the fire and passion in her voice when she'd talked about the homeless kids, he'd have wondered if there was ice-water instead of red blood flowing through her veins.

It was only too obvious she didn't feel the same fire and passion for him—which was just as well, given the way things were going in his business and the things he hadn't told her.

'Mike!'

Something in her voice suggested it wasn't the first time she'd said his name, and he glanced behind him to see Marco hovering there.

'Sorry, Marco, I was thinking of something else. Real menus tonight?'

'Tonight I have a real chef,' Marco said, his brown eyes twinkling in welcome. 'Sundays, I do the cooking myself. You'll have a drink while you consider what to eat?'

Once again, Jacinta ordered a small glass of dry white wine and Mike, though tempted to ask her to share a bottle of wine, decided to stick to light beer. He really did want to talk about the problems of over-prescribing, and his head was already fogged by Jacinta's sudden incursion into his life.

But sitting with her, seeing her across the table from him, filled him with a nameless pleasure. Had he felt the same way—in this same booth—with Lauren all those years ago?

He searched both mind and heart, but couldn't remember—certainly couldn't recall a warm sense of fulfilment like the one he was experiencing now.

A warm sense of *fulfilment*? When Jacinta had just told him she had no intention of investing her time or energy in him? Was he going mad?

Fortunately a waiter appeared with their drinks and hovered, waiting to take their orders, so Mike broke the silence by asking what she'd fancy, and by the time the waiter departed he'd managed to get his mind back in order. The rest of him would surely follow.

'Prescriptions—that's what we were talking about when you suggested dinner. I've just remembered.' Jacinta smiled with such delight he wondered if she, too, had been thinking thoughts she'd rather not have thought. 'Something to do with Rohan's patients.'

It was important, he reminded himself, but once again he stalled, only this time it was professional discretion that made him hesitate.

'Let's forget Rohan's patients for a moment, and discuss over-prescribing in general.' That sounded about as business-like as he could get! 'How can it be monitored?'

'It's already checked, to a certain extent, by the government regulatory bodies,' she reminded him. 'Through pharmacy records. But within clinics such as yours?'

She tilted her head to one side and he immediately recalled her description of herself as a 'little brown mouse'. There might be something mouse-like in that particular gesture but, from what he'd seen of her, a lion would have been closer to the mark—make that lioness, given both her gender and the mile-wide protective streak she seemed to have.

'It's probably time all prescriptions were computer-generated. I understand they are in some of your clinics, but at Abbott Road we're still in the Dark Ages. If they were computer-generated, and all the computers linked to a central system, then it would be easy enough for a programmer to set up something that would automatically scan and monitor the prescribing of all drugs, or specifically chosen drugs, or whatever you happened to programme it to do.'

Mike nodded, pleased she'd diverted him with her common sense.

'All the individual office computers are already linked, but we've only computerised the patient files and script generation in the two most recently opened clinics.'

He smiled at her.

'You're right—about Abbott Road *and* about how easy it would be to keep an eye out for the dangers of over-prescribing.'

Now was the time to tell her about selling Abbott Road, but she was smiling back at him, and he didn't want to see that smile fade.

Particularly didn't want to see the anger he knew would spark in her eyes.

Not tonight.

So he talked about the people at the meeting, then asked how she'd persuaded so many government employees to become involved.

'Most of them really care about the work they do—or they did when they first began in their positions. But they become swamped in the paperwork, and office politics, and the business side of things, and lose sight of the people. Coming to the "Optional Extras" meetings brought them back in touch with the reality of homeless youth.'

'They met some of the people to whom their funding goes,' Mike said. 'Makes sense to me, but they still have their paperwork to do—surely they can't find time to attend your meetings on a weekly basis?'

Jacinta's smile grew perceptibly brighter, as if his interest were a gift.

'It's not every week—we don't meet on the first Tuesday of the month. You could use that night for CPR lectures if you wanted. You haven't forgotten them?'

He hadn't, neither had he done any more about it, in spite of the death of the man they'd tried to save still weighing so heavily on his mind. But before he could bring up the subject, Jacinta was speaking again.

'The meetings differ. Tonight the focus was on permanent accommodation, so all the people involved in that, right through to a member of the Minister's staff, attend. The third Tuesday in the month is always on training and education so, as well as kids who are interested in furthering their education, we get a range of teachers and career specialists and guidance officers from various high schools and day and evening colleges. We get people in to talk about what they do as well, from plumbers to university professors.'

'And the fourth Tuesday?' Mike asked, fascinated by what was being achieved in evening meetings at his old clinic.

Another smile flashed his way.

'Mainly for kids—it's form-filling night. How to apply for anything from youth allowance to admission to one of the private colleges now offering scholarships to these kids. A lot of social workers and psychologists come along so it's developed into a bit of a group therapy night as well. The kids can have a one-on-one chat with someone if they have specific problems, or they can bring up their problems in a general forum and have everyone discuss it. We seem to hug each other a lot on the fourth Tuesday.'

Mike made another mental note—'Attend meeting on the fourth Tuesday.' Even if he didn't get to hug Jacinta, he could check on who else might be doing it.

'Does it worry you so much, using the clinic waiting room for these meetings?'

The question startled him.

'Worry me? Not at all. I'm surprised by how much you've achieved, but not worried.'

'Then why are you frowning?'

He'd have liked to have said he wasn't, but undoubtedly she had seen a frown or she wouldn't have asked the question.

But he didn't want to think, let alone admit, that the thought of Jacinta hugging someone made him frown. Hugs were fairly impersonal after all.

'You're doing it again,' she told him. 'Something's obviously bugging you.'

Fortunately, their meals arrived at that moment, so Mike was able to turn the conversation to food.

Which was delicious, Jacinta admitted to herself, pleased she'd resisted pizza earlier. But something she'd said had aggravated Mike. Though she'd been quite rude to him about 'investing in a relationship', he hadn't seemed to take offence, and she'd been able to relax and enjoy his company and their conversation.

Until he'd frowned.

She selected another mouthful of food then glanced across at him. A little shadow of the frown remained, though he did seem to be enjoying his meal.

A strong face, with a good bone structure...

He caught her staring.

'Do I pass muster?' he asked, and she hoped she didn't look as embarrassed as she felt.

'Actually, I was thinking what a good skull you must have—under the hair and skin and flesh.'

His shout of laughter rang out, causing heads to turn their way, while Jacinta squirmed with even more embarrassment that she'd blurted out the first thing to come into her head.

'I suppose I should be grateful you're thinking about me at all,' he said, when his laughter had died down to occasional chuckles. 'But a skull? Did you have murder on your mind?'

No way! But she could hardly tell him that attraction had led her to the comment, when she'd been adamant she wasn't interested in having fun with him.

'You'd be the one more likely to be thinking murder,' she replied. 'It was wrong of me to use the clinic after hours for meetings, but I did try to contact you for permission.'

His chuckles died away and the frown returned.

'Am I really so inaccessible?'

Jacinta nodded, pleased she had a mouthful of food and wouldn't be expected to reply. There'd been nothing inaccessible about him earlier, when he'd kissed her...

She cut another piece of chicken and added a small sliver of mushroom to her fork, then glanced up at him.

He was watching *her* this time, and something in his eyes suggested he might also be thinking of the kiss.

Jacinta felt her nipples peak, pressing almost painfully against the lace of her bra. She wanted to rub them, to ease the tension his look had caused, but a strange lethargy was stealing over her, weighing her body down with the heaviness of desire.

'Maybe I could afford just a little time for fun,' she muttered, only realising the words had been loud enough for Mike to hear when his eyes lit up and his lips—those, oh, so kissable lips—tilted into a smile.

'I hope that muttered remark wasn't connected to your "lame ducks".'

'That remark was my subconscious taking over.' Jacinta tried valiantly to regain lost ground. 'Doesn't mean a thing!'

'No?'

The inflection in the word, uttered in that dark gravelly voice, sent feathery ripples of sensation down her spine. Tingles tangled with them and her body thrummed with such anticipatory pleasure she looked around, wondering if anyone had noticed this almost silent seduction.

'Are you ready to go?'

Jacinta nodded, then shook her head. She was about to say she hadn't finished her meal when she realised she must have pushed her plate away earlier. It was definitely gone—taken no doubt, while other appetites ran riot through her body.

'Sure you wouldn't like dessert? Another glass of wine? Coffee?'

The booth was too dimly lit for Jacinta to see the expression in his eyes, but she was reasonably sure there was a teasing subtext to the words. The wretch knew exactly how she was feeling. Knew she needed fresh night air to cool the burning in her body.

'No, that was lovely, thank you,' she said politely, though right now she couldn't remember what she'd eaten.

'Then shall we go?' he murmured, rising to his feet and holding out his hand.

She slipped her fingers into his—aware that this was the

physical equivalent of standing on a diving board, about to plunge into her fantasy volcano.

Pheonixes rose from ashes, she reminded herself as she followed him through the throng of people near the bar and out the door into the night-time quiet of the mall.

And fire regenerates much of the Australian bush.

Could she look on it as a regeneration?

He didn't break into her silent debate with words, though he did tuck her hand into the crook of his elbow and hold it there so her body was drawn closer. As well as peaking nipples, she now had breasts aching with a longing she'd forgotten existed.

Then Mike turned down a side street, startling her into an awareness of where they were. He must have felt her hesitation for he said, 'I thought as both our cars were in the car park off the lane, we'd walk this way. Do you need to go back into the clinic for something?'

My common sense? My determination not to get involved with you?

Not things you could bottle to take as cures or preventatives, she knew, so she shook her head and kept walking in step with him while his body whispered silent messages to hers and she wondered if people ever screamed aloud with frustration.

They rounded the corner into the lane, lit here and there but still sufficiently shadowed that a couple of steps took them into a patch of darkness.

'Thank heavens,' Mike whispered, turning her so their bodies faced each other. 'I'd never have made it back to the cars.'

And with a hunger that matched what she'd heard in his voice, he put his arms around her, drew her close and bent to kiss her.

Lights like fireworks exploded in her head, and she clung to him, exploring his mouth, his tongue, his cheeks, his chin and neck with kisses eager for as much sensory knowledge of him as she could gain through lips on skin.

'Bloody hell, Jacinta Ford, do you have any idea what you do to me?'

Actually, being so close, she had a pretty good idea. She just couldn't find the breath to speak so once again she nodded, then realised she shouldn't have—much too forward when she barely knew the man—so she shook her head, before allowing him to put his arm around her shoulders and steer her down the lane.

What on earth was she doing?

'No, it's no good!' she mumbled. 'Apart from anything else, I just don't have time for an affair right now. I've got too much on, with ''Optional Extras'' still getting off the ground, the new house about to open and the ''Kids Helping Kids'' thing starting to happen...'

She must have betrayed her agitation in more than the words for once again he eased her to a standstill and turned her into his arms, restarting the fireworks with his demanding kiss.

But why give in to those demands?

The whisper was so weak Jacinta managed to avoid it, and plunged into the volcano once again.

It took for ever, but they reached the car park eventually, and the sensor lights flooded their two cars, the sudden brilliance making Jacinta pull away from Mike's body—but only slightly. If she pulled away too far she'd probably collapse, given the way her knees were trembling.

'We'll go in my car,' he announced, speaking for the first time since he'd asked his question.

'Go where?' Jacinta asked, though what she should have said was no.

'To your place, of course,' he said, while his car flashed lights and made a noise to indicate he'd unlocked it. 'I'd take you to mine,' he added, opening the passenger side door while retaining his firm grip on Jacinta, 'but my father lives with me and he never goes to bed before midnight and he'd be sure to ask questions that would probably embarrass you.'

In what way? Jacinta wanted to ask, but the 'to your place' thing had better be sorted out first.

'I live at home—I mean, where I've always lived—with my mother.'

Mike stared at her in disbelief.

'You still live at home? With your mother?'

It was the incredulity that did it.

'Well, you still live with your father,' Jacinta snapped at him, ducking out from under his encircling arm and marching across to unlock her own car. Though, of course, she needed keys and they were somewhere in the bottom of her handbag. If she could only train herself to put them in the same compartment every time! 'Bloody hell!'

'My sentiments exactly. In fact, I used it first!'

She looked up from her scrabbling to find Mike standing behind her, and the funny little smile playing around his lips made her ache to nestle back into his arms—though in a less sexual way than she'd nestled earlier.

'I suppose it *is* funny,' she admitted, finally finding the keys and unlocking the car door. 'Though the fact that we both have inconvenient parents might be for the best. It wasn't ever going to be a good idea, was it, Mike?'

Sadness washed away the last flickerings of the heat of her desire.

She's right, Mike's head told his body. In fact, a relationship with her would be darned inconvenient.

And very short term, given his accountant's news about selling Abbott Road and Jacinta's likely reaction to it.

'I'm going back to my real job tomorrow and, though we didn't get around to discussing your ideas on cost-cutting, I've spoken to Carmel about running the place with just two doctors. She thinks it will work, if only on a temporary basis.'

Jacinta's head dipped forward, and the silky hair swung down to hide whatever expression was on her face. But the gesture spoke of disappointment—because of the downsizing of the clinic or because she wouldn't be seeing him the following day?

He reached out and brushed his hand across her hair.

'I'll phone you,' he found himself promising, 'and I'll also make sure every one of my "minions" as you call them, knows you're to be put through to me at any time.'

Mike slipped his fingers under her chin and tilted her head up so she had to look at him.

'This isn't goodbye,' he added softly, then, ignoring the warnings of consequences which his head was yelling at him, he bent and kissed her gently on the lips.

Felt the tremble in the so soft flesh and heard the whisper of a sigh before she kissed him back.

'My father might have gone to bed,' he muttered gruffly, when she eased herself away from his body, leaving him feel more frustrated than he'd been through all his recent months— years by now—of celibacy.

But Jacinta was having none of him.

'Even if it was a good idea—which it isn't—it's too soon. But now you know I work for you, maybe I'll see you around some time.'

Her small shoulders lifted in a slight shrug, the movement reminding him how fragile her bones had felt when he'd grasped those shoulders earlier. A small, neat, compact package, but with a fire that he suspected had already singed him.

He touched his finger to her nose.

'Goodnight, then, little brown mouse.'

Ha! Tempted out a smile!

'Goodnight, boss!' she responded, getting her own back on him.

He held the car door for her, closed it, then waited while she started the engine, backed out and drove swiftly up the lane. The temptation to follow her—to perhaps catch a glimpse of her as she alighted from her car—was so strong it shocked him back to reality.

She was right. Getting involved was *not* a good idea. Virtually impossible, given both their circumstances. Jacinta Ford was not the kind of woman one could take to a hotel room for a quick couple of hours, neither did he think she'd take kindly to him setting her up in an apartment somewhere.

But as he drove home his mind ranged through the apartments he owned. Places he'd bought as investments.

He could say he'd shifted into one of them...

If one happened to be unleased at present...

Made a mental note not only to check out investment apartment leases but to take more control of his own affairs.

He parked the car, locked the garage and walked into the house through the kitchen, where his father was sitting at the table, book propped against the sugar basin, enjoying a cup of tea.

He crossed 'Check out apartment leases' off the list, as his father asked, 'Been out with Jaclyn?'

'Jacinta,' Mike corrected automatically, thinking more that he couldn't leave his father to rattle around in this big house on his own.

'Jacinta? Got a new one or did I get the name wrong? Surely you're not taking out a Jaclyn and a Jacinta at the same time? Seems risky to me, lad. The names are way too close.'

Mike found himself smiling at his father, though if there was anything even vaguely amusing about the situation with Jacinta, he had yet to find it.

'Actually, it was business.' More or less! 'She's the doctor I was telling you about. The one who insisted I go back to Abbott Road.'

'Not a bad idea, going back to your beginnings now and then,' his father said, but his eyes were straying to the book and Mike knew that for once he could escape further questioning.

The prospect of going to work lacked its usual delight for Jacinta, and she snuggled deeper into her mattress, trying to bury memories of the previous evening.

'I'm off,' she heard her mother call, and though she knew Fizzy was in the house, no doubt asleep now daylight hours had come, Jacinta felt an aloneness as if the house had emptied of all life and, in doing so, had emptied her as well.

'Stuff and nonsense!' she muttered, forcing herself out of the bed and into the shower. 'Ridiculous fancies!'

Then, because these mutterings didn't seem to be doing any good, she dredged up an old expletive from her teenage years and tried that instead.

But it lacked the sense of daring it had provided back then, so she dressed and went grumpily down the stairs to the kitchen, cheering up only when she saw Fizzy wasn't still sleeping but was in the process of cooking what looked like a delicious breakfast.

'I asked your mother about your favourite foods,' she said shyly. 'You've been so good to me—to all of us. I cooked bacon and pancakes and there's maple syrup and also some hash browns. I cheated with them and bought some frozen ones yesterday, but your mother said they were very good.'

Jacinta crossed the room to kiss their visitor, while the day grew noticeably brighter.

This was the kind of reward she wanted from what she did in life. OK, a little sexual gratification might be all right, but to give up the time she spent helping Fizzy and others like her to do a bit of lotus-eating with Mike Trent?

She sat down at the table, all doubts banished, and tucked into the kind of breakfast she only dreamed about these days. Just lately, even at weekends, there'd been no time for indulgences like cooked breakfasts.

Fizzy sat opposite her.

'I've talked to your mother about the baby and all that. It was best, wasn't it?'

'Not necessarily best,' Jacinta said slowly, aware that Fizzy's emotional state must still be precarious and picking her way through the minefield. 'But perhaps meant to happen. If you'd gone on to have the baby, going back to school when the new term starts would have been difficult. And with the others at school, you'd have been lonely during the day. Babies aren't a lot of company, you know.'

'Just a lot of work,' Fizzy said, and Jacinta knew some of her mother's words had struck home.

'Exactly.'

'If I do really well at school, do you think I can go to university? Mrs Ford was saying the course she did isn't difficult, and it'd be wicked to think I could do stuff like she does with other kids. I mean, I've been there, haven't I? So they'd have to listen to me.'

Jacinta chuckled at the girl's determination.

'They certainly would,' she agreed, and thanked heaven, and her mother, that Fizzy seemed to be looking so positively towards the future.

'It's only the school. Whether we'll get one of those counsellors who want to do a family mediation thing.'

Aha! Was that what the breakfast was about?

Jacinta glanced at her watch and decided the clinic wouldn't fall apart if she was ten minutes late.

'For a number of kids, getting them back with their families is the best option,' she said. 'And in a lot of cases, the social workers are so overloaded they don't go into a particular situation carefully enough, which happened when the social worker at the hospital contacted your mother. They mean well.'

'Yeah!'

Nothing she could say was going to convince Fizzy, so Jacinta moved on.

'As far as school's concerned, you've already met the principal and the student guidance officers, and they know a little of your background. I doubt you'll get pressure from them, but if you do at any time, you've a good back-up team behind you now. You'll have Dave and Helen, the house-parents at Ellerslie House, and me and Mum for use in emergencies. If anyone hassles you, walk away—politely. Say you'd like to think about it and get back-up before you have to see the person again.'

'That sounds OK, but will I be able to do it?'

Jacinta smiled at her.

'Or will instinct take over and you'll run? Is that what's worrying you?'

Fizzy nodded.

'Well, at least you have a choice of places to run to now,' Jacinta reminded her. 'The clinic, this house, Mum's office, or your new house. You don't know Dave and Helen well now, but they're wonderful people, there to support you in whatever way they can.'

She finished her meal while Fizzy chatted about her plans for the day—a shopping expedition with the other young people who'd be shifting into the house to choose furnishings for their bedrooms.

'Now, *that* I'd love to join,' she told Fizzy, 'but only as an onlooker. Poor Bonnie, who'll have to keep you all within budget, not to mention the limits of good taste.'

'You're late!' Carmel's greeting was to be expected. Jacinta *was* late, but only by about five minutes. 'And we're going to be on a very tight schedule as we've only two doctors.'

Jacinta nodded. She was too busy battling a jumble of sensations—a vague feeling of loss that Mike wasn't there, a memory of that first unexpected, unasked-for but mind-blowing kiss and a twinge of regret for the way the evening had ended—to argue with Carmel.

She went into her consulting room and within minutes was calling her first patient.

'I thought it was just the flu but when I got into work I felt much worse,' Ken, an office worker from across the mall, told her. 'There's a couple of us haven't been the best, so whatever it is must be very catching. I know Pat Richards came to see one of the doctors yesterday.'

Pat Richards! Mike had seen him but had asked Jacinta's advice. She'd suggested a chest X-ray for the hacking cough and possible admission to hospital for further tests. But had Pat gone to the hospital?

'I don't think you should be at work,' she told Ken. 'You've a high fever, there's obviously congestion in your chest and you certainly won't be much use except as a carrier of infection—which your colleagues won't want.'

'Will you give me a certificate?' It was the usual question, though this time Jacinta would be pleased to provide it.

'Of course, and also a referral for a chest X-ray. You should get that done today on your way home. Have you a local doctor, someone near your home? I could get the results sent to him or her.'

Ken provided the name and address of his local GP, took the medical certificate, thanked her and departed, but Jacinta watched him go with an uneasy feeling in the pit of her stomach. It was late summer—not the time of the year you'd expect to see many cases of flu or pneumonia.

If Abbott Road's patient files had been computerised, she could have looked up Pat Richards and seen whether Mike had suggested hospitalisation. She could still do it later.

Her next patient was a regular. Jenny Tinsley worked in the pharmacy next door to the Abbott Road building. She was happily pregnant with her first child, and in for her regular antenatal check. Jacinta felt a twinge of envy, and knew it was a biological reaction—a reminder that the urge to procreate was wired into her system.

An image of Mike Trent flashed obligingly into her head, and she shivered.

'Don't tell me you're getting this summer flu that's going around,' Jenny said, as Jacinta pronounced herself satisfied with the foetal development and helped Jenny off the examination table.

'Have you noticed a lot of it?' Jacinta asked, thinking that Ken and Pat were the only patients the clinic had seen, then realising that Mark or Rohan could easily have seen others.

'More than you'd expect for this time of the year,' Jenny told her. 'Though I guess with air-conditioning in all the city buildings it spreads easily.'

Jacinta had her doubts about influenza spreading through air-conditioning, thinking it more likely that people sneezed on each other, but the mention of air-conditioning re-awoke the uneasiness she'd felt earlier. In spite of frequent and compulsory checking of air-conditioning plants, Legionnaires' disease, an often deadly lung contagion spread through some air-conditioning plants, was becoming more common. If there was a problem with the cooling plant in the building across the road...

Jacinta had no time to pursue her worries until early afternoon, when she took a break to eat a sandwich and grab a cup of coffee, using the time without patients to find Pat Richards's file.

Mike had recommended hospitalisation for Pat, and Jacinta, checking his personal details, found a home number and dialled it.

A woman answered, explaining she was Mrs Richards's mother and, yes, Pat had been admitted to hospital. She named a large private hospital on the outskirts of the city, but didn't know the name of the doctor treating Pat.

Jacinta thanked her for the information, and was in turn thanked for caring enough to follow up on a patient's visit. Not wanting to worry the family unnecessarily, Jacinta accepted her thanks and hung up.

She phoned the hospital, and was finally put through to Pat Richards's ward, but the sister there referred her to the specialist who was in charge of the case.

Muttering to herself about patient privacy and the limiting features of something she usually upheld rigorously, she found the specialist's number and dialled his office.

'He's doing rounds at the public hospital at the moment,' an obliging receptionist told her. 'But I'll leave him a message to say you called.'

Jacinta left her work and home numbers, then added, 'Could you tell him it's urgent?'

No doubt she'd earn his ire if it turned out to be a false alarm, but if Legionnaires' disease was spreading through the building across the road, the sooner the air-conditioning plant was closed down and checked, the better.

By six-thirty, when she was preparing to leave, the specialist still hadn't called. She tried the private hospital again and had him paged, but with no result. She unlocked the reception area, thinking there might be a file somewhere with a home number for the man, but the specialists' file gave the number as unlisted.

'I already knew that,' she said crossly to herself. 'The damn man's probably out having an after-work drink with colleagues or playing cricket in his back yard with his kids.'

She heard a door close but thought it must be Tim, Mark's counterpart, leaving, so it wasn't till she heard his voice that she realised Mike was not only in the room but had heard her complaints.

'Don't you ever go home?' he asked, moving easily towards her. 'And did you know that talking to yourself is a sure sign of frustration?'

'Of course I'm frustrated!' she informed him, while excitement battled warnings that being excited was wrong, wrong, wrong. 'But not the way you're thinking, thank you very much. Would you believe I've been trying since early afternoon to get in touch with this wretched man, and will he phone me back?'

Mike stopped moving but, although he was at least two metres away, he was still too close.

'What wretched man?'

Jacinta named the specialist and Mike grinned.

'If I solve your problem, will you have dinner with me?' he teased, pulling a minute mobile phone from his trouser pocket and pushing a couple of the buttons. 'Rick's number is programmed into this. His daughter is a great friend of Libby's so I keep the number to check on the kids' social engagements when Libby's home.'

'Sorry to bother you at home, mate, but one of my clinic doctors would like a quick word.'

He passed the phone to Jacinta with the air of a magician producing a rabbit out of a hat. Once again she was overwhelmed by a jumble of emotions, not least of which was delight at seeing him again. Not a good feeling, given all the reasons she shouldn't fall in love with Mike.

'It's Pat Richards, your patient at Waratah Private,' she said.

'I've another patient who works with Pat and is showing similar symptoms. Sick last week and put it down to flu, but today had a temp of forty degrees, shivery, dry, unproductive cough. Then one of the salesgirls from the pharmacy spoke of a lot of summer flu going around. Pat's building is across the street from the clinic and the pharmacy and, while it might be nothing more than a virulent flu, I wondered if you'd tested Pat for Legionnaires'?'

The specialist swore. 'His X-rays showed enough abnormality in the lungs to keep him hospitalised. We've been treating him for pyogenic bacterial pneumonia and I've ordered cultures of lung tissues to be sure. But cultures will take days to grow. The tests on his pleural fluids were positive, but they can show a false positive with legionella. The only true test is on a lung biopsy. Actually, I can go back and arrange that and a urine test right now. If we get even a suspicion of legionella infection, I can get the Health Department onto it immediately. It will be up to them to check the air-conditioning system and take the necessary steps to prevent the infection spreading.'

A sudden cessation of noise told her he'd hung up.

'Is he onto it?' Mike asked.

'I assume so,' Jacinta said. 'Not one for social niceties, is he?'

Mike smiled at her.

'You probably shook him up,' he said, his gaze roving across her face. 'Seems you have the ability to do that to some men.'

CHAPTER EIGHT

'SO, DINNER?'

Jacinta stared at Mike. She was still getting over his last comment. And his presence in the clinic.

'I've got to get on to my patient first,' she said, dashing back into the back of the reception area and taking refuge behind the patient files. Ken! Ken who? Work, mind, work!

But how could her mind work when Mike had followed her into the filing area? When he was touching her shoulders, turning her to face him, tilting up her chin?

'I've got to find Ken,' she said, though she was trembling from her own eagerness for the kiss she knew was coming.

'So find him,' Mike challenged. 'I'll help.

He turned her back to face the files but stood close, one hand resting lightly in the small of her back. Not only was her mind not working, but she doubted if she'd have the strength to reach up for a file—if she ever recalled Ken's surname.

'He'd be in the appointment book,' she muttered to herself, but instead of turning away from Mike to go and look it up, she turned into him, so once again had to exert a supreme effort of will to move at all.

Ken Hemmings. Of course. Back to the files where, naturally, the Hs were on the shelf she couldn't reach. Ignoring Mike, she kicked the little wheeled stool into place and clambered up.

Halstead, Ham, Hatfield, Head, Hemmings.

She grabbed the file and was about to jump down from her perch, when Mike caught her by the waist, and swung her to the floor, dropping a swift kiss on her lips en route.

'You're being very silly about this,' she told him, trying to sound stern when what she really felt was a shivery excitement. 'I don't want to get involved with you at all, and though I might have weakened, just slightly, last night, and briefly considered a quick fling type of thing with you, we both realised that's impossible, given our living arrangements.'

She'd have managed stern quite well if Mike hadn't started smiling at her halfway through her little speech. The smile had made her voice go wobbly, no doubt due to the fact that her lungs weren't working properly.

A situation that hadn't improve when he continued to smile, and even agreed with her.

'I know,' he said, his voice seeming deeper than ever. 'But if I promise not to touch you again, will you do whatever you have to do for Ken, then come and eat with me?'

'What about your father? Doesn't he expect you to eat at home occasionally?'

He was standing beside her as she dialled Ken's number, and she asked the question as she waited for someone to answer.

'Only breakfast. He cooks that for me himself. But in the evenings…'

Mike shrugged, and Jacinta remembered how his shoulders had looked without the shirt.

'You're usually out with a woman,' she finished for him. 'The lovely blonde?'

That scored a scowl.

'I'm usually working late. I work long hours. It goes with the territory and is probably why my marriage failed and another reason why I don't want to get into a situation like that again.'

Jacinta was grateful for the timely reminder that any relationship with Mike would be purely short term and the emotional risk all hers, as he obviously found such arrangements quite satisfactory.

'I don't think anyone's at home,' he said, and she was so lost in the process of weighing up the emotional risk in a relationship with Mike that she didn't understand him.

He took the receiver from her hand and set it down, then tapped the file.

'Write down the number and you can try later,' he suggested. 'From the restaurant. I booked at Tivoli on the off-chance you'd say yes.'

Tivoli—it was the newest, most talked-about restaurant in the city.

'Why are you doing this?' Jacinta demanded, as a sudden urge to give in to him startled her with its strength.

'Asking you to dinner?'

He sounded so innocent she scowled at him.

'Pursuing me like this. It's bad enough that I don't want to get involved with you and I've told you so, but if you add to it that I'm certainly not your type, then why the persistence?'

His smile this time was less certain. A little lopsided, and decidedly tentative.

'I think it must be the kisses,' he said, shrugging again. 'Believe me, I've asked myself the same question a dozen times today, asked it the whole time I was driving over. I've so much worked piled up I should be in my office—probably till midnight—but, no, here I am. It has to be the kisses. It's all I can put it down to.'

Jacinta shook her head.

'You're mad—do you know that? Crazy. At what stage did you make a booking at Tivoli—or do you have regular bookings made at a number of restaurants in case you get the urge to wine and dine one of your women?'

He gave an exasperated growl and moved towards her, but she ducked out of his way.

'You make it sound as if I keep a stable full of women—which isn't true. One woman at a time has always been my motto—heavens, one woman's enough trouble for any man!'

'Then what about Jaclyn? Isn't she the one of the moment? And in that case, what am I? Just a kiss-receiver? A small glitch in the one-woman-at-a-time-and-nothing-lasts-for-ever scenario?'

The growl deepened and this time, as he moved towards

her, she didn't duck in time. He grasped her shoulders and pulled her close, bending to kiss her with such deliberation she knew she'd pushed him too far.

His mouth burned against hers, so when he slid his tongue across her lips she welcomed the cool relief of it. Her body strained closer to him as if it needed to be totally entwined in, or engulfed by, his. The small cry of pleasure pain that eased from her lips seemed to encourage him, and his kisses became more heated and far more demanding.

Why are you doing this? Jacinta's question was hammering in Mike's head, but all he could find by way of a reply was that he couldn't stop himself. Any more than he'd been able to stop himself coming over here this afternoon—leaving it as late as possible in the hope she might have left work, then driving like a madman because he'd feared he might miss her.

'It might be addiction,' he offered, when they'd stopped to draw breath and he'd slumped back against the reception counter, his arms still enfolding the source of his problems in his arms. 'If I'd ever kissed you with lipstick on, I'd have to think it was something in the colour, but as it's been nothing, or paint, on those tempting lips so far, I can only think it's a chemical thing. Caffeine-treated perspiration, heroin-tainted lips.'

The little chuckle she gave moved her breasts against his chest. She was all softness, this small woman, so cuddly he didn't want to let her go.

'Or maybe I've reverted to childhood,' he added, thinking of a small bear he'd cuddled in much the same way.

'Were you into kissing back then?' she asked, looking up at him so he felt himself drawn into the depths of her dark eyes. Thoughts of drowning flicked briefly through his mind, then returned as a possible explanation for his erratic behaviour. Which was ridiculous!

'You keep kissing me back,' he pointed out, hoping to get past the question by turning responsibility back to her.

'That's because I've enjoyed it,' she admitted, then she grinned as he'd obviously revealed his surprise at her honesty.

'Well, I have,' she added with a touch of defiance. 'But you shouldn't take too much of the credit. It's been a long time since I've done any serious kissing, so there's a certain novelty value in it.'

'Novelty value? You certainly know how to reduce a man to nothingness, don't you?'

Jacinta smiled at him, not in delight at scoring but with such genuine warmth his heart felt as if a band were tightening around it. This phenomenon, more than anything else, warned him he was treading on dangerous ground. Playing around with a woman who could affect your heart was surely a precursor to rethinking the not-getting-married-again decree.

But if his business was so important, why wasn't he in the office right now?

Maybe...

Mike smiled back and saw the glimmer of light in her eyes as her own smile broadened.

'Shall we go to dinner, then?' he murmured, knowing he'd kiss her again if they didn't move soon.

Say no! Jacinta's head ordered, but her lips just kept smiling at the wretched man and then her head nodded.

'I'll try Ken again first and phone home to tell Mum I'll be late.'

'Or even later?' Mike said, glancing at his watch as she moved out of his encircling arms. He looked surprised to find it was close to eight. 'Wouldn't you normally be home by now? Or are you usually at work until this time?'

She grinned at him as she dialled.

'I earn every bit of the money you pay me, boss!'

You shouldn't be teasing him *or* going out to dinner with him! her head continued to nag.

But her heart knew if—when—he kissed her again, she'd kiss him back.

Still no answer at Ken's place, so she phoned her mother, got her own voice on the answering machine, telling her she couldn't come to the phone right now, and left a message, simply saying she'd be late.

'I'm glad you didn't say how late,' Mike murmured. He was standing behind her, not holding or touching her but so close she could feel her body tightening in response to his.

She wanted to ask why, but decided she didn't want to know. No matter how much she might wish for the physical release of sexual pleasure with Mike, she didn't want to think he'd asked her to dinner just to get her into a bed.

Any bed!

Although that's the way he plays the game, she reminded herself. He's already told you that.

Once again the 'will I, won't I' debate started up in her head, but the sexual excitement he'd generated in her body was superseding all other thoughts and emotions and she knew beyond doubt that, should he ask, she'd certainly be tempted.

So much for all your good intentions, her head muttered glumly. And your bold talk of 'investing time and emotion in a relationship'. You're as bad as a giddy schoolgirl on a first date.

'Yes,' she admitted, answering the internal voices and startling Mike at the same time.

'Did I ask something, or were you anticipating the question?' he said, then, as he bent forward, his lips seeking hers with the unerring accuracy of a heat-seeking missile, he added, 'But having been given permission, I can hardly resist.'

She responded again. Possibly with too much fervour, for this time when they stopped to breathe he muttered, 'Let's go. Right now! If we stay here any longer I'll be ravishing you on an examination couch and, believe me, I'm too old for that kind of sexual gymnastics.'

The words shook Jacinta as much as the kiss had, but she knew he was right. If they didn't get out of the place, there was no knowing what might happen.

'I'll take my car. That way I can drive home straight from the restaurant.' She was finally listening to the dictates of her head, though it was hard to concentrate on the instructions. Lock up carefully because, for all the kisses, that's the boss standing there. 'Besides, if we both get into yours we probably won't get out of the car park.'

She smiled as she said it, knowing it was an admission to match the one he'd made earlier.

Mike shook his head, as if not knowing how to take her.

Or perhaps he was as puzzled—no, make that dumb-founded—as she was by the attraction that had flared between them.

'Of all the unlikely situations,' he muttered, showing he was in tune with her thoughts. 'OK, we'll take two cars.'

'I'll follow you,' she insisted, not because she didn't know the way but because she was reasonably certain she'd muff her gear changes, or forget to turn on her lights, or do some-thing equally stupid if he was right behind her. Just thinking of him following her sent shivers up and down her spine—not of fear, unfortunately, but more like physical delight.

They reached the restaurant, parked side by side in a hedged area beside it, then Mike opened Jacinta's car door, and took her hand to help her out.

As they walked towards the low-set building, hand in hand, Jacinta felt a special sense of belonging that she realised im-mediately was far more dangerous than her physical responses to Mike.

'Ah, Dr Trent.' The major-domo greeted Mike with too much familiarity. 'I have put you on the small veranda.'

Fighting a nagging peevishness over Mike being here with other women—of course he would have been—she allowed herself to be led to the 'small veranda'.

It was like a low balcony off the main dining area, protrud-ing out into the lushness of the garden, with the river below them, gliding darkly and mysteriously by on its passage to the sea. Light flickered from tall cane lamps burning among the bushes, and the sweet scent of ginger blossoms suggested a plant flowering nearby.

'It's lovely,' Jacinta admitted when the man had seated them, left menus and departed.

'It is nice, isn't it?' Mike said, looking around as if to take it all in. 'I've not been out here before. When Dad and I brought Libby here a few weeks ago, we sat inside.'

Foolish relief swamped Jacinta, so suddenly and deeply that she knew whatever she was feeling for Mike had gone beyond simple attraction. Gone beyond magnetic attraction, too, for that matter.

Panic fluttered in her heart, and to douse it she thought of work.

'I should try Ken—if you don't mind me using your mobile,' she said.

Mike passed the tiny phone to her, and showed her how to open it. Their fingers brushed against each other's, tangled for a moment, then held, and she looked up into his eyes, blue-grey tonight and soft with a longing that left her breathless.

'It's important,' she managed to say.

He released her fingers and the phone immediately, but what she'd seen in that unguarded moment had shaken her.

Ken's wife answered.

'Pat Richards's wife phoned me from the hospital when the specialist went back there,' she said when Jacinta had explained who she was and why she'd called. 'Pat knew Ken was feeling off last week—they'd sympathised with each other. The specialist waited at the hospital until I got there with Ken. He's having the same tests, but I had no one to mind the kids so had to take them with us, and now I've just got back.'

'Do you mind if I keep in touch? I'd like to know how things go.'

The woman assured Jacinta she could phone any time.

'If I'm here, I'm here,' she said.

Jacinta thanked her and ended the call, then passed the phone back to Mike.

'What's up now?' he asked.

Startled by the question, she glanced across the table at him. 'Why should something be up?' she countered, and saw his smile light up his eyes.

'Because the menu can't possibly be bad enough to have caused the frown you gave it.'

'Did I?'

Jacinta studied him a little longer, thinking not about her reply but how unusual it was to have someone noticing her frowns—perhaps caring how she felt.

Her mother did, of course, but this was different.

Very different.

'I was thinking how hard it must be for a woman with young children to juggle them and hospital visits when her husband is ill. Wondering if Mrs Hemming has relatives who'll help her.'

'More lame ducks, Jacinta?' Mike said, but his voice was soft, as if her caring had somehow touched him.

'Those ones are definitely not my responsibility,' she said, 'though I do hope she has good support. She sounded quite cheerful, and apparently your specialist friend was very positive about good outcomes for patients where Legionaires' disease is detected early.'

'He's a top man,' Mike assured her, effectively ending the conversation.

Jacinta turned her attention back to the menu.

'Far too many choices,' she said. 'How can anyone possibly decide when there's so much on offer?'

Mike smiled at her and she knew he'd put a different twist on her words.

'What do you like?' he asked, so huskily she felt tremors in her knees.

'In the way of food, I meant,' he added, his eyes twinkling at her obvious confusion.

'Small meals,' Jacinta said, determined to take control of the situation. 'I might have two entrées.'

'An intriguing idea,' Mike murmured, and the trembles worked their way down to her tingling toes, while the perfume in the air seemed to intensify, causing further chaos to her senses.

'Stop right now!' Jacinta told him. 'There are so many reasons why we shouldn't be considering a relationship, I don't know why I said yes to dinner.'

She gave him what she hoped was a stern look, then remembered and went on, 'Actually, I do. You bribed me.'

'And you wouldn't have come otherwise?'

She gave up on the menu and studied his face once again. Almost straight black brows above the silvery eyes, a nose that balanced the no-nonsense chin. Cheekbones so sharp they might have been cut by a sculptor's knife, the lot enhanced by taut, lightly tanned skin.

You skipped the lips, a voice whispered in her head.

And shall continue to do so, she told it.

A good-looking man, she mentally summed up, but not stunningly so—not so magnetic that women fell at his feet in droves. Though they probably did, but his money would help there.

'Finished?'

Mike saw her flush and wondered just what she'd been thinking. Jacinta's dark eyes had scanned his face with the intensity of a skin specialist seeking out any lurking cancers.

Was it because he couldn't guess at her thoughts that he found her so intriguing?

'I think I'll have the Thai-style prawns first and then a small Tandoori pizza,' she said, ignoring the other implications of the question, though her eyes told him she knew exactly what he'd meant.

He found himself smiling again, a genuine, heartfelt smile because he was enjoying himself—enjoying the way the conversation ducked and weaved while the undertones of their unexpected attraction for each other coloured nearly every word.

'Why did you expand? Go from hands-on medicine at Abbott Road to big business?'

The waiter had taken their orders and departed, and Mike had been about to point out a full moon, rising slowly behind the houses across the river.

So much for romance!

But the question made him think back.

'Had you always intended to open more than one?' Jacinta prompted.

'No,' he said, because that was easy to answer. 'When I started Abbott Road, I thought that's where I'd stay. Chris Welsh came in with me almost from the beginning, and the practice was profitable for both of us. As it grew we had to take on someone else, and suddenly three doctors were making nearly twice as much as two because we didn't have to increase office staff.'

'So the spectre of great wealth to be made raised its tempting head?'

Jacinta spoke lightly but Mike sensed disapproval in her voice—or maybe he imagined he did.

'I guess so, though I didn't ever consider "great wealth" a goal. A secure income was more important,' he admitted. 'And though so many people seem to think making money is immoral, providing one isn't hurting anyone in doing it, surely it should be seen as admirable.'

'Which it is,' Jacinta agreed, and he peered suspiciously across the table at her.

Jacinta Ford agreeing with him?

Fearing hidden sarcasm in the remark, he found himself explaining.

'All the clinics we set up were in new areas. There were no existing medical services so no one was put out of business. Forest Glen was different—it's an older suburb but experiencing a lot of growth so the existing services couldn't cope.'

'I'm not criticising you, just wondering why the switch from medicine to business. Medicine's not an easy profession to get into, given all the study required, and to give it up after that... I just wondered if perhaps you didn't enjoy it. If you found it too limiting.'

It was Mike's turn to study her. Intent brown eyes fixed on his, the creamy skin and soft pink lips framed by the silky, shiny dark hair that fell so neatly—sweetly—down across her ears.

'I'm sure I didn't find it limiting. In fact, the time I've spent at Abbott Road has reminded me of how much I enjoyed hands-on medicine. But things just grew, and as the clinics expanded, the business needed someone to look ahead—to consider the options for further expansion.'

He paused, wondering if she'd understand or if admitting the force which had driven him would put her off him for ever.

Which wouldn't be a bad idea, his conscience suggested. Given what you've yet to tell her.

'You see, part of me had always wanted to establish a base of long-term financial security. Not so much for myself, but for Dad and for any children I might have. My father was a clever boy, topped his class at school, could have been anything, but the family wasn't well off and he had to leave school early to help support them. He went into the mines, in the days when most miners worked underground and didn't earn a lot of money. My mother died when I was two—'

'Two? How on earth did your father manage working with a two-year-old?'

'His mother helped, and my mother's mother, minding me when Dad was on shift, but when I was growing up it seemed as if he was always there. And his dream was for me to have the education he'd missed out on.'

Mike saw Jacinta smile and cocked an eyebrow at her.

'What?'

'Did he want you to have it for the sake of learning, Mike, or so you'd make a lot of money?'

In spite of the smile, her voice was soft with understanding. Which, contrarily, made him feel worse, not better.

'What is it with you?' Mike demanded. 'You have an uncanny knack of firing your sharp little arrows right through whatever weak defences I might have erected. Of course he wanted me to have the learning, but that didn't stop me wanting to repay him—to make enough money so he'd be comfortable for the rest of his life.'

'I can understand that,' Jacinta assured. 'And is he?'

'Most definitely,' Mike told her. 'He was injured in a mine accident while I was still at university, and lost the use of his legs, but during a long stay in hospital and an even longer convalescence he became a voracious reader. Something he hadn't had time to do before. Now, as long as I keep up my library stocks, he's happy.'

Mine accident! Mike had said the words so calmly, but Jacinta could imagine the churning terror that must have struck the young student Mike had been. She'd seen the scenes on television—desperate family members clustered by the top of a shaft, not knowing what the rescuers might find. She could picture Mike there, unable to help, imagining the death of his sole parent. Then rescue, and again the waiting, this time for a verdict—life or death—and finally the reality of the man who'd done so much for him coming through it all, but no longer the strong and active one in their relationship.

She reached out and took his hand, and brushed her thumb across the backs of his fingers.

'I'd have wanted to give him the world,' she said softly, as this revealing insight into the man she'd labelled a materialistic entrepreneur made her feel closer to the person behind the legend.

The arrival of their first courses brought the revelations—and the hand-holding—to an end, but Jacinta felt as if Mike, in revealing this sketchy fragment of his past, had bestowed a gift on her.

And in doing so had shifted the parameters of their relationship.

Her head got into the act again, telling her such thinking was fanciful nonsense, then the subtle but delicious flavours of the food demanded more attention and she gave herself over to the sensory delights of eating.

'Enjoying it?'

Mike's smiling comment reminded her of his presence—though she hadn't totally forgotten him.

'Very much so,' she said. 'I love food. No doubt I'll end up the size of a house—a small house—if I ever stop working, and having to run around frantically when I'm not working, to catch up with my life.'

'And people label me a workaholic!' he teased. He seemed about to add more when a muted sound made him reach for his pocket and extract his mobile.

He held it to his ear, and his eyes flicked towards Jacinta.

'Yes, she's here. I'll put her on.'

The thoracic specialist she'd spoken to earlier explained that Pat's urine test had been positive for Legionnaires' disease. Although that was a quick early way of getting a positive diagnosis, further tests would be needed for one hundred per cent identification.

'We're looking at your other patient now, but I wanted to thank you and also ask you to alert the other doctors in your practice to the situation. If they've any doubts about any patient, please, refer them to me. I've contacted the Health Department and they'll test the building's air-conditioning. In fact, someone's probably onto it already.'

Jacinta thanked him for phoning, but he insisted it was he who was thankful.

'We should get together,' he added. 'Get Mike to bring you around some time.'

It was a simple remark, and didn't mean the specialist was thinking of Jacinta as anything other than one of Mike's colleagues, but the warmth she'd felt earlier—the belonging she'd felt with her hand in his—dissipated. She doubted whether she'd be in his life long enough to be introduced to his friends, and if she was—if such a thing did happen—wouldn't the inevitable parting be even harder?

'Was it bad news?' Mike asked as she passed the phone back to him.

'No,' she said honestly. It had been her decision to have dinner with him, not the news, which had been bad. 'At least now someone's doing something before more people are affected.'

'So you should look happy. After all, you began the alert.'

She tried a smile but felt it wobble on her lips.

'Yes, I should, shouldn't I?'

CHAPTER NINE

'THERE'S a path down to the river if you'd like a short walk,' Mike said, when Jacinta had refused coffee and he'd paid the bill. 'Libby found it last time we were here.'

Mike took her hand and led her through the dining room and out a door. The setting, and the scene before her, especially now the moon had got into the act, was so romantic it was easy to imagine they were the only two people in the world. Yet doubt and sadness, in equal measure, had wormed their way into Jacinta's heart.

He'd told her about his father, mentioned his daughter often in his conversation, yet even if she became more involved with him she'd never be part of these people's lives. And now she knew a little of his history, she could understand his unwillingness to risk his father's security.

Honestly, Jacinta, her head muttered at her. You've known the man less than a fortnight and you're worrying because a relationship with him might be short term. And *you* talked to *him* about expecting relationships to fail! Take a hint from the river—go with the flow, enjoy whatever you can get out of it then move on.

But her heart knew it wasn't that easy. Time made no difference. What she felt for Mike had already gone beyond physical attraction.

'Figured it out yet?' he asked, the huskiness of his voice causing the goose-bumps to pucker her skin.

'No,' she answered honestly, wondering if she was always so transparent or if Mike saw things others didn't see.

'Maybe a kiss will help,' he suggested, guiding her into a fern-shaded grotto by the river.

A kiss will seal my fate, she thought, then wondered if it

136

was a quotation she'd heard or read somewhere as it seemed an unlikely thought to be having.

But while her head puzzled over its own words, her body was revelling in the way Mike's hands brushed across her skin, the way his fingers lingered in specific spots—beneath her ear, above the pulse in her wrist.

His touch was priming her for what was coming, and she let him touch her. Her nerves and sinews tightened in expectation, her mouth felt dry and pebbled nipples brushed against the confines of her bra.

So when he finally gathered her close and pressed his lips to hers, she responded with all the fire he'd built inside her and gave herself up to the multitude of sensations just kissing him provoked.

'I think this grotto is an even worse place than an examination table to be making love to you,' he muttered when, this time, she disengaged her lips and moved far enough apart to draw in some much-needed air.

'Are you busy this weekend? Painting walls somewhere?'

Jacinta knew what he was asking, but the kiss had, as promised, already sealed her fate.

'I'm working Saturday morning and, no, being the boss doesn't mean you can change my duty hours. But after that...'

She should be out at the new house, helping the kids, volunteers and the new house-parents set it up for the big opening. They'd barely started on the gardens. Or she should be catching up with her mother, whom she'd seen more at meetings than at home lately. Or—

'Then I'll pick you up after work and we'll go up the coast. Or would you prefer the mountains—one of those cabins in the hills, where the owners provide hampers of food and perfect privacy? Name the place you'd like to go.'

Jacinta felt his words surge over her like a tidal wave, tossing and tumbling her until decision-making was impossible.

'You decide,' she managed to say, before he kissed her to seal the agreement.

*   *   *

In the cool light of day, the idea was, of course, ridiculous. Jacinta arrived at work wondering if Mike's promise that she'd always be able to contact him held true. She'd find out when she phoned him later—in the first break between patients.

Or maybe at lunchtime, though he could have a business lunch so not be available.

She worked her way through the usual stream of minor illnesses, injuries and assorted pain, and between patients argued ceaselessly with herself.

'Without an X-ray it's impossible to tell how badly affected the joint is, Mrs Nevin,' she said. 'X-rays these days aren't harmful, and as you're on a pension you can have it done at the radiology clinic for nothing.'

'What makes you think I'm on a pension, young lady?'

Mrs Nevin's querulous demand startled Jacinta.

'Aren't you on a pension?' she asked, looking more intently at the elderly woman, clad in threadbare rags and, as usual, clutching an armful of plastic bags bulging with an assortment of equally threadbare garments.

'I wouldn't take money from the government if they paid me to!'

Pale blue eyes darted fire at Jacinta, daring her to ask more.

A dare she set aside for the moment.

'If you're not on a pension, you can have a free X-ray at the hospital,' she suggested.

'I don't need a free anything, young lady, so don't patronise me! I can pay for an X-ray if I want one, but I don't. Nasty things, those X-rays. They do more damage to your insides than you doctors let on. If God had meant us to know what was going on in our bodies, he'd have given us transparent skin, now, wouldn't he?'

'I guess so.' Jacinta found herself agreeing, though weakly. Transparent skin? The image it threw up was horrifying!

'But,' she said, rallying again, 'you could get rid of the pain in your hip for ever with a hip replacement. Wouldn't it be worth having an X-ray to see if it would be an appropriate treatment?'

'Have someone else's hip in my body? No thank you!'

Jacinta wondered just how badly she'd muffed the beginning of this consultation to have Mrs Nevin thinking this way. She sorted through a drawer, found a picture of a metal hip prosthesis and began again, explaining hip-replacement options to her patient.

'I'd rather have the pain,' Mrs Nevin told her. 'If you could just make my tablets a bit stronger, then it wouldn't be so bad.'

She struggled to her feet, collected up her plastic bags and prepared to leave, but every time she moved Jacinta saw the wince of pain imperfectly concealed.

'Here's a prescription for a different type of anti-inflammatory tablet that might help with the pain.' She handed the slip of paper to Mrs Nevin. 'Sometimes changing tablets works for a while. But, please, come back and see me soon. We'll talk again about what can be done.'

Mrs Nevin shot her a doubtful look, as if by even mentioning hip replacement Jacinta had somehow let her down.

She opened the door to let her patient out, and realised she wouldn't need to phone Mike. He was there, over by the reception desk, chatting to Carmel as if he popped in every day.

He nodded to Jacinta then, as she pulled the next patient card from the box and was about to call the patient's name— at least she'd achieved something this week—he held up his hand, said something to Carmel and crossed the distance between the reception area and Jacinta's consulting room with long, sure, determined strides.

Bemused by both his unexpected appearance and her own reaction to it, she stood aside to let him in. He closed the door behind him, reached for her, then rested his back against the door while he kissed her with such ruthless intensity she had to bite back little cries of...

Ecstasy? Surely not.

Submission?

Her?

'You're driving me mad, do you know that?' Mike's demand put her own problems out of her head. 'I couldn't wait until Saturday. Damn it! I couldn't even get through a whole day. I have architectural plans to study, a backlog of financial papers so high I can't see over them, decisions to make about the expansion, and all I can think about is a little brown mouse with lips that send me wild and a body I long to ravish so thoroughly we might have to stay in bed for a year.'

He looked down at her, his eyes steely grey, alight with what she suspected might be passion, then growled, 'Well, don't you have anything to say for yourself?'

'I've a patient waiting. We're short-staffed, remember.' Jacinta was pleased to hear that her voice was shaking only slightly. Boy, was she handling this well! Like a mature, sensible adult, in fact. 'And while we're on the subject—' when on a roll one might as well keep going '—it would make more sense to cut back on the associated medical personnel—nurses—and the office staff, if you need the clinic to be more financially viable. Somewhere along the way, we were going to discuss this, but you keep letting the sex thing get in the way.'

'*I* keep letting the sex thing get in the way?' he growled. 'You're the one who keeps kissing me back.'

'But only because you're there—or should that be here?' Uh-oh! She was losing it again. Perhaps because he was smiling at her, and the tip of his forefinger was running up and down the inner surface of her forearm and driving her to distraction.

'I've a patient waiting,' she repeated, only far more weakly, when the glint in his eyes told her he was about to kiss her again.

'And I've got work to do. One last quick kiss, small mouse, then I'll see you midday Saturday.'

He stole the kiss before she could object again—stole her breath as well, so when she did re-emerge from her room, several minutes after Mike had departed, she could barely make the patient's name heard above the hubbub of the waiting room.

You didn't tell him you wouldn't go away for the weekend, Jacinta was thinking while Carol Speares, who worked with Ken and Pat in the building across the road, poured out her concerns about working in the contaminated building.

'It's a strange thing, but not everyone breathing the same air is affected,' Jacinta explained, forcing herself to concentrate on her job. 'I guess it's like viral diseases that sweep through an office but only some people catch them. The tests the Health Department is organising for you to undergo will be conclusive, Carol. And they'll be followed up after a month with retesting.'

'But I want to have a baby,' Carol told her. 'We talked about it—about me going off the Pill—last time I was in, but with this hanging over my head...'

'You don't have any symptoms of Legionnaires' disease, but you'll know for sure when the test results come back—in about ten days maximum. You could put off the plans for getting pregnant for ten days, couldn't you?'

'But I'm already off the pill. We've been having sex and I might be pregnant already. *And* have the disease!'

Carol was sufficiently distressed to totally distract Jacinta's mind from thoughts of Mike—though she did tuck the word 'Pill', with a question mark behind it, to the back of her mind. To be retrieved and considered later.

She unlocked the cabinet with her illicit supply of free samples and sorted through it.

'Let's start with a pregnancy test. Here's a test kit—the instructions are on it. I'll give you two, in fact, as it's early days yet and it mightn't be showing in your urine. In the meantime, until you're cleared, use protection. I'm sure your husband will understand the need for it until you know for certain that you're OK.'

Carol took the test kits and thanked Jacinta, but she was still disturbed and Jacinta felt a niggling sense of doubt that, had she not had her own personal life on her mind, she might have provided a better service for her patient.

Perhaps going away with Mike for the weekend was the

answer. It would get the sex over and done with and she could then get back to normal.

Brave thoughts indeed, but did she believe them?

'Mr Warren?'

A tall gangling youth rose from a chair and walked towards her. His pupils were so dilated that, except for a rim of colour at the very edge of the irises, his eyes looked black.

She led him into her room, conscious, as she always was with addicts, that she had to be on full alert.

Particularly today, when distraction came so easily.

'What can I do for you?' she asked him as he slumped into the chair.

'Get me off the stuff. Do something, anything, but if I don't get off, it's going to kill me.'

It was the voice of despair but sometimes, just sometimes, an addict meant it and was willing—or desperate enough—to go through the rigours of a detox programme.

'Have you tried before?' Jacinta asked, while she riffled through papers on her desk for the phone number of the nearest drug rehab centre.

The young man nodded.

'Been on meths, it didn't work. Want naltrexone. Implants. That's what's working.'

On some addicts, though it's still not fully tested—not even legal, Jacinta thought, while she wondered what she could say that would keep him interested in seeking help.

'We can't do that here. You need a place where you can be treated and remain for a while after treatment. I can phone Freedom House, and ask someone to pick you up from here. They can offer you all the available options and look after you while you come off it.'

Her patient shook his head.

'I've been there, they don't do it, but someone said the clinic does it.'

A cold dread clutched at Jacinta's heart. Could one of the other doctors in the clinic be illegally implanting naltrexone?

If the practice was even suspected, the Medical Ethics Board would have reason to shut down the clinic.

Mike Trent wanted the place shut down...

Don't go there, her head warned.

'Well, I don't,' Jacinta said, when she realised she hadn't answered Mr Warren's assertion. Couldn't keep calling him Mr Warren either. She checked his card. 'Brad, I'm sorry, but until the implants have been properly tested, they *are* illegal. And if you find a doctor willing to do it, he's practising beyond the law and there could be serious consequences for you as well as for him. It's not yet approved because no one's sure how it's going to affect patients long term. As a drug, it affects the liver, so if you've a hepatitis infection, or any problems with your liver, it could kill you.'

He leapt from his chair so suddenly that Jacinta felt a flicker of fear. She poised her knee just below the panic button on the underside of the desk, ready to press upward if she needed help.

'Do you think this is better than being dead?' Brad leaned across the desk, supporting his weight on hands bunched into fists.

He thrust his face towards her.

'Look at my eyes. What do you see? Emptiness. Nothing. That's what you see. That's my life. Nothing.'

He stormed towards the door, but Jacinta followed him and caught at his arm.

'But it doesn't have to be that way, Brad. Give ordinary rehab another go. The programmes are better now, they've houses in other places where you can live while you're recovering. You can get out of the cycle you're stuck in. It can happen!'

She spoke with all the passion that had brought her to work in this place, and something must have got through because he slumped against the door, where another man had leant so recently, and nodded at her.

'Can you ring them? Ask them to pick me up here? I'll wait

in the waiting room. If I go back outside I'll see someone I shouldn't and before I know it I'll be planning another score.'

'I'll arrange it for you,' Jacinta told him, speaking gently so she didn't frighten him away. 'Sit down for a minute. I'll get someone to take you into the treatment room and make you a cup of tea while you're waiting.'

She phoned Reception first and asked for Jenny, who was the most empathetic of the associated medical personnel, then phoned the rehab centre and quickly explained, knowing the time when an addict felt strongly about seeking help was limited. In another hour Brad might have lost the urge which, this time, might save his life.

But the reminder of why she was so committed to Abbott Road stayed with her, blocking out her fantasies of making love with Mike, shutting memories of his kisses into a compartment way back in her mind.

Where it had to stay if she was going to be an effective doctor, she told herself as she drove home, deliberately going out of her way so she could pass the Tivoli and remember their dinner together.

So her head scoffed at her heart, and altogether she was more muddled than ever.

'You look exhausted,' her mother scolded, when she walked into the house and dropped her bag on the floor in the front entry.

'I think I might be,' she replied, 'though a quick bath will revive me. I'll be down in time to sample whatever delicious food it is I can smell.'

Guilt hit her like an added weight on her shoulders.

'It was my turn to cook last night, wasn't it? I didn't give it a thought.'

'Fizzy and I managed on our own—went to the bistro down the road, in fact. But we were pleased to think you might be doing something nice for yourself for a change.'

Boy! Wait until these well-meaning folk heard about the plans for the weekend!

Now was the time to tell them.

At least tell her mother.

'I won't be long in the bath,' she said, shirking the reve-
lation, mainly because she was still wondering if she could
shirk the arrangement as well.

And if it would be for the best if she did.

'So what's he like? Tell all,' Fizzy prompted when, clad in
her second-oldest jeans—the oldest being covered in paint—
and a loose sloppy sweaty, wet hair clinging limply around
her face, Jacinta came down to dinner.

'What's who like?' she asked blandly, though she knew she
wouldn't get away with it.

Couldn't help but smile either, just thinking about Mike.

Perhaps she wouldn't cancel the weekend.

'Good-looking, tall, we look stupid together, grey in his
hair, he's thirty-eight, divorced, twelve-year-old daughter I
presume lives with her mother, and he won't ever marry again
so I shouldn't get involved.'

'Oh, dear,' her mother said. 'You've fallen in love with him,
haven't you?'

Jacinta eyed her with suspicion, mentally replaying what
she'd said.

'How on earth can you reach such a conclusion from that
description? We look ridiculous together.'

'There you go again,' her mother said. 'If you weren't in
love, you wouldn't care how you looked with him.'

Jacinta threw her hands up in the air.

'I d-don't b-believe this!' she stuttered. Then she frowned
at her mother. 'And what makes you such an expert anyway?'
she asked. 'You've had any number of men following you
around like lovesick chooks—'

'Roosters?' Fizzy suggested helpfully.

'Well, roosters, then—for years. Since Dad died, in fact.
And have you ever looked at one of them? What do you know
about love?'

Her mother smiled.

'I knew it with your father—right from our first meeting. I

guess I'm just a ''on love in a lifetime'' person, though if it happened again at least I'd recognise it.'

'You're saying I wouldn't?' Jacinta demanded, unable to believe she was having this conversation but unwilling to let it drop.

'I'm saying you're often too committed to what you're doing to give it a chance. Fire and passion are tremendous assets in any job, but they can also burn you if they're not put to proper use. Maybe some of it could be channelled into a relationship.'

Where it might totally consume me, Jacinta thought, remembering the volcano.

'I'll get our meals,' Fizzy offered, while Jacinta reached out and took her mother's hand.

'I know what you're saying, Mum,' she whispered. 'I guess what worries me is that I might also be a ''one love in a lifetime'' person as well.'

'And you're afraid of getting hurt? Anything worth having carries the risk of pain, Jacinta. From birth onwards. And you've never been one who stood fearfully on the sidelines of life. You've always plunged right in.'

But into volcanoes?

She shook away the question and smiled at her mother.

'I'm going away with him for the weekend,' she said, dismissing all her own doubts in that simple declaration. Then she tucked her mother's hand into her arm and they walked through to the kitchen, where Fizzy was setting out their meals on the big central table.

Fizzy demanded more information, but Jacinta turned the conversation to the new house and the furniture-shopping expedition.

'I felt bad,' Fizzy said, 'buying all that stuff. I don't think Mum ever had anything new.'

Jacinta heard the loss and longing in her voice and hoped that one day Fizzy and her mother could be reconciled. As her own mother asked more questions about the house, Jacinta considered the bond that existed in families, even abusive ones.

Then felt a momentary wave of guilt that she wouldn't be around to help with the final preparations for the grand opening the following weekend.

The loud demands of the phone interrupted both her thoughts and the conversation.

'Do you want to get that, Fizz?' Jacinta suggested, thinking she could delay standing up for another few minutes. Evening phone calls were usually for her, and usually a crisis of some kind.

Fizzy returned with a huge grin plastered across her face.

'It's *him*!' she announced, as if Jacinta had won the lottery with a personal phone call. She was waving the cordless receiver in her hand. 'You *will* take it here, won't you?' she teased.

Jacinta grabbed the phone from her and carried it with her out the back door.

Her greeting was so tentative it was a wonder Mike heard it, but he must have for suddenly he was speaking, the deep voice sounding even deeper on the phone.

'I did something I've never done before and pulled an employee's personnel file to get your home number. Then, blow me, if you don't live just two streets away from me. Do you want me to come over?'

'To meet my family? Chat to Mum and Fizzy?'

She heard his husky chuckle.

'Not exactly what I had in mind but, yes, if it's what I have to do to see you.'

'You saw me earlier today,' she reminded him, while her heartbeats rattled against her chest in excitement. Such silly behaviour could only be love. Couldn't it?

'It wasn't enough,' he was saying. 'Look, I can walk over. Maybe we could sit in your garden and talk. I can't picture the house. You *do* have a garden, don't you?'

'Sit in the garden and talk?' Jacinta repeated, putting enough emphasis on the last word for him to get her drift.

'Whatever! Shall I come?'

She looked out across the garden, saw the moon coming up on the eastern horizon and sighed.

'No. I'm really tired and need to get a good night's sleep, and "talking" to you isn't conducive to good nights' sleeps.'

There was silence—long enough for her to wonder if anyone had ever said no to Mike Trent before.

'I'll accept that excuse,' he said at last, 'pathetic though it is. But only on condition I can see you tomorrow night.'

'What about the piles of work you're neglecting, the architect's plans, the billion-dollar business?'

'It's going to hell in a handcart,' he told her, 'and it's all your fault. But now that I've seen my dad and you've turned me down, I'll scoot back to the office and put in a good few hours. I *will* see you tomorrow?'

'I'm working late—the clinic's open till eight on Fridays—and by the time I pack up, it's always after nine and I'm always tired, cranky and terrible company.'

'Then I'll pick you up and spirit you away to somewhere special. Trust me.'

Jacinta heard herself agreeing then, to make matters worse, indulging in the kind of silly conversations lovers had. And smiling as she did it.

Her head had apparently given up on convincing her of the folly of this relationship. In fact, the way she was carrying on, her brain must have taken leave of absence.

'You should have asked him over,' her mother said, when she finished the conversation and walked back inside. 'He lives not far from here.'

'How do you know that?' Jacinta demanded. 'You haven't been checking up on him, have you?'

Her mother smiled.

'Of course not, but I see his father at the shops from time to time. Ted Trent. I didn't put the two of them together until yesterday when Ted and I were talking about broccoli and he was saying how it had taken him years to get his son, Mike, to eat it.'

'You talk to this man about broccoli?'

Jacinta felt as if the world had suddenly tipped sideways, causing separate bits of her life to collide.

'Not always about broccoli,' her mother replied. 'But we chat. He's reading Aristotle at the moment and I did ancient Greek at school, so he was asking—'

'Don't tell me,' Jacinta said. 'I really don't need any more confusion in my life. I'll do the dishes as I didn't cook, then I'm off to bed.'

But sleep wouldn't come, held at bay by thoughts she didn't want to have. It was all very well to contemplate an affair with Mike—to be adult and mature about it because she knew it wasn't going anywhere permanent. He'd made that clear from the start. No marriage—not even a long-term commitment, Jacinta suspected, as that could be as financially dicey as marriage.

Which was OK for him, but what about her? Could she have that kind of relationship with him? Could she find joy in something that held, from the beginning, no promise of a future? And if she could, at what cost would it be to her emotional well-being when they parted? Would she be able to pretend she didn't care when her mother said, 'I saw Ted at the shops today'? Would she be able to not ask, 'How's Mike?'

She'd phone him in the morning. Stop the nonsense before it went any further. Better now than later.

Still muttering clichés, Jacinta drifted off to sleep, awakening not to the same determination but to a skittery excitement that she'd be seeing him that evening.

'You're hopeless,' she told herself as she showered and shampooed her hair—twice.

'Weak,' she scolded as she pulled clean underwear, trousers and a cotton knit sweater from her wardrobe and tucked them into a plastic bag with toiletries and make-up.

'And you'll regret it!' she warned, as she all but danced down the stairs.

'I'm on late tonight and might go somewhere with Mike

when I finish,' she told her mother, who was sitting over coffee in the kitchen. Then, deciding some things were best not talked about, she dropped a kiss on her mother's head and added, 'I'm off. I've heaps to do. I'll eat at work.'

Her mother eyed the plastic bag but didn't comment, merely saying, 'We'll see you when we see you, then.' She turned back to the paper.

But Jacinta knew her lips were smiling, and a new worry loomed. She should tell her mother right now there was nothing in this fling with Mike, so she didn't start thinking in terms of wedding plans and grandchildren.

But such a confession would reveal too much—draw judgement on Jacinta's own behaviour, though doubtless it would remain unspoken. Her mother had always let her make her own mistakes.

By the time Jacinta finished work, the tumult in her mind had added to the physical tiredness a long day always caused, so she felt, and no doubt looked, like a piece of chewed string.

She eyed the plastic bag, trying to summon up the energy to walk through to the washroom, have a quick wash and change her clothes. The idea had all the appeal of pulling out her toenails.

A light tap on the door made her straighten in her chair. Please, let it be Carmel saying goodnight, not another patient.

'Come in,' she said, and heard the lack of welcome in the words, so when the door opened and Mike poked his head around it, she didn't quite know how to react.

'Poor mouse,' he said. 'You look exhausted. Are you finished? Can I take you away from all this?'

'Are you sure you want to?' she asked, as his gentle solicitude weakened whatever feeble defences she might have retained. 'Look at me. I did intend washing and changing, but somehow the effort's got beyond me. Did Carmel tell you about the baby we had?'

Mike beamed at her.

'Trent Clinics' first on-the-spot delivery. You all did very well. Carmel says they wanted to call the little girl Jacinta after you.'

'Poor child. She'll have people asking how to spell it all her life.'

'So, shall I carry you out to the car?'

Jacinta looked at him then—really looked at him—and caught what could almost be uncertainty in the lines on his face.

And because uncertainty seemed such a strange thing to associate with Mike Trent, she smiled and stood up and said, 'Oh, I think I'll manage the distance. But first I'll have a wash, even if I don't change.'

She'd barely finished speaking when doubts assailed her.

'But perhaps I should change. Where are we going?'

'No, you don't need to change, and it's a surprise. Just relax and go with the flow.'

'But my car...'

He reached out and put his finger against her lips, touching her for the first time and firing her nerves once again to tingling anticipation.

'We can leave it there. Now I know where you live, I can pick you up in the morning and drop you at work.' Mike paused, studying her, then added, 'No, I was going to do that anyway so your car wasn't sitting here over the weekend. What we'll do...'

It was her turn to touch his lips.

'Let's forget the car thing. I often catch the train so there's no need for you to pick me up tomorrow. Mum and I will come in together and she can take my car home.'

Without thinking, Jacinta had offered him a cue—a chance to say he'd pick them both up—but he didn't take it. And though a wedge of sadness forced its sharp point into Jacinta's heart, it didn't stop her body responding to the kiss he dropped on her lips. Neither did it stop her kissing him back, when he took her in his arms and drew her closer.

CHAPTER TEN

MIKE drove along the freeway, glad the traffic had thinned and he didn't need to give one hundred per cent of his attention to the road. He knew the way to his destination well enough to give at least forty per cent to his passenger, who'd slid into the leather seat beside him, murmured something about comfort, then promptly fallen asleep.

He glanced Jacinta's way and realised he needed more than forty per cent of his attention to work out what was happening between them. Was he heading for a mid-life crisis that he'd suddenly become besotted by this woman? To the extent that his work was suffering? That he'd phoned Jaclyn within twenty-four hours of meeting Jacinta and told her—gently, he hoped—he wouldn't be seeing her any more?

That he wanted, more than anything, to introduce Jacinta to his father?

Yet all the while he knew a relationship between them wouldn't work. If his insistence that their affair was only temporary didn't kill whatever it was they had going, then selling the Abbott Road building surely would.

He had to tell her, and the best time to do it would be tonight. But could he do it?

Jacinta slept without moving until he pulled the car off the road and rolled it forward to where it offered the best view out over the city. The moonlight shining through the windscreen gleamed on her hair, and made her small face look pale.

There was an innocence about her as she slept, which was so at odds with the passion of her kisses that his body tightened with desire for the other surprises she might offer.

As if sensing his watchfulness, she stirred and opened her

eyes, seeing him first then, as she straightened, the glittering lights of the city below them.

'It's like a scattering of jewels flung across a dark bed-spread,' she murmured, peering out towards the lights. 'Are we on Mount Merion? I've been here by day for picnics, but never at night.'

Mike felt a jolt of pleasure at her transparent delight, and wondered if she could read it in his foolish smile.

'I have a picnic basket, rugs and cushions. Will you join me, my lady, on the grass?'

'Oh, Mike, this is wonderful! I never dreamt...'

She leaned across and kissed him on the cheek—a kiss of thanks, but so infinitely sweet he wondered if he'd ever felt so happy.

Of course he must have done, he told himself as he gathered gear from the boot of the car. Think of the pleasure you've had from the success of the business.

But he pressed his fingers to his cheek, touching the skin she'd kissed, and wondered if pleasure and happiness were the same thing. If they were, perhaps satisfaction was a better word to describe the emotion his business brought him. And even that had waned considerably lately.

'Can I carry something? You don't have to do the lot.'

Jacinta stood on the other side of the boot and reached in for a blanket. It was such a homely kind of gesture somehow. He could picture her doing it in years to come, pulling out a child's stroller, some toys and then the hamper.

It *had* to be a mid-life crisis.

He shook his head and found she'd gone, no doubt to spread the blanket. He grabbed the hamper, promising himself he'd think about the crisis tomorrow.

'There's wine—I brought both red and white—and finger food, which I hope is easier to eat than knife-and-fork stuff.'

He was almost stuttering again in his efforts to sound nor-mal, so he took a deep breath, told himself to calm down and set the basket on the blanket. Went back for cushions and returned to find Jacinta had set out plates and napkins, glasses and a bottle of mineral water. She'd even opened the wine.

'Sit,' she said to him, 'and tell me about this place. I can't see any picnic tables. Is it a public park?'

So he told her how he'd bought the ten-hectare block many years ago, intending one day to build a weekender on it, but somehow work had taken over his life and he'd not got around to it.

'But it's such a beautiful place. By day, you'd see right out to the ocean.'

She leaned across to offer him a tiny pastry, holding it to his lips so he could take a bite.

Then he fed her in turn and slowly but surely the meal became a prelude to seduction. A kind of foreplay so exciting he could barely breathe by the time they'd finished strawberries dipped in chocolate, and she invited him to lick the remnants off her lips.

'Are you sure?' he asked, knowing she'd know exactly what he meant.

'I'm sure,' she murmured, and lay back against the cushions, slowly slipping undone the buttons on her sensible shirt so he could see tantalising glimpses of the lacy bra and creamy breasts beneath it.

'You're beautiful, Jacinta Ford, do you know that?' he whispered, brushing the dark hair back from her face so the moonlight could shine on her features. 'For all you put yourself down with talk of small brown mice, you've an inner beauty that comes through like a special radiance.'

'You're not so bad yourself,' she said softly, fending off embarrassment by turning the compliment back on him. Her dainty fingers traced his cheek, his nose. 'Great bones—but I told you that before.'

He chuckled, surprised to find there was so much pleasure in prolonging even more the delights that lay ahead.

'The skull?'

Her smile widened and her fingers moved to his lips, tracing their outline, her forefinger probing towards his teeth.

He bit the invader, but gently, then kissed her wrist and set it down on the blanket above her head, joining it with its mate then holding them gently so she need have no fear, while his free hand pushed aside the open shirt and his fingers slid beneath the lace.

Jacinta felt her breath catch, and though she strained against his hold she didn't try to break it. Instinct told her she was safe with this man, whose intention, she knew for certain, was to give as well as to receive pleasure.

'Moonlight on Jacinta,' he murmured, finding and releasing the catch at the front of her bra then pushing it back so she lay near naked from the waist up, and open to his scrutiny. 'So beautiful!'

His hand brushed across her breasts, then held one, as if to test its weight. His little finger curled upward to tease at her nipple and the whisper of sound that erupted from her lips was a plea, not a protest.

Mike responded with his lips, feasting first on one, and then the other rosy, peaking breast, until Jacinta broke his grasp and put her arms around him, holding him close yet uncertain how best to ease the longing he was creating.

She slid her fingers beneath his shirt, heard a button pop and in the end demanded parity.

'Let's both get naked and we'll start again,' she suggested, and smiled to see the startled look in Mike's eyes. 'That is where we're heading, isn't it?' she added, snuggling up to him so her naked breasts rubbed against his shirt.

'As soon as possible,' he managed to reply, and the hoarseness of his voice suggested he'd been holding himself on a tight rein, determined to put her pleasure before his own.

But still he teased her, and she teased him in turn until, when neither of them was willing to wait a moment longer, he entered her, sweetly and gently, holding her as if she were the most precious thing in the world, murmuring words of pleasure, asking, encouraging, until they found each other's rhythm and joined in celebration of the mutual delights of love.

Later, sated, he held her still, tucked against his body so he was a source of both warmth and protection. His finger traced her contours, face, breasts and belly, while his lips smiled down at her and his eyes, even in the moonlight, held a wonder she suspected was reflected in her own.

There were no words, no more chat, just contentment so deep Jacinta wondered how she'd lived without it. It was only when the night breeze sprang up and she shivered that he moved, handing her her clothes, helping her with buttons while she offered help to him. Silence lay between them, as comfortable and easy, as natural as the moonlight that wrapped them in its glow.

They packed up and drove back to the city, Jacinta's hand pressed against Mike's leg, a sense of destiny—of belonging to this man—so deep within her she was certain everything would work out in the end.

'Until tomorrow, mouse,' he whispered, kissing her one final time in the front doorway of her home. 'And over the weekend, we'll talk about the future, because leaving you like this is agony. I want you tucked up beside me as I sleep, not two streets away!'

'Me, too,' Jacinta agreed sleepily.

She waited by the door until his taillights disappeared from sight, then made her way inside, walking slowly up the stairs to her bedroom while her mind replayed the special highlights of a very special evening.

The alarm broke into Jacinta's deep and dreamless sleep, and though she longed to lie in bed a little longer and relive the memories of the previous night, her mother's voice reminded her they had a train to catch.

And she had a bag to pack, though she'd forgotten to ask Mike if they were going to the mountains or the beach.

'Though I doubt it will matter,' she muttered to herself as again she threw clean underwear into an overnight case. 'The way things are we probably won't get out of bed.'

The thought sent the tingles up her spine and heat into her

lower abdomen, so she had to hug herself to still the excited stuttering of her heart.

Somehow she got through breakfast, parried her mother's questions about the previous evening and arrived safely at work. Now, surely her mind would settle into work mode and take her body with it. A bit of 'sensible' was what she needed here.

As the only doctor on duty, she was busy, which was good, though her eyes kept straying to the clock. Saturdays were often chaotic, so chances were she wouldn't finish work until late. Knowing that, Jacinta had arranged to phone Mike before her last patient.

But as twelve o'clock approached, the plan fell to pieces. Norrie Clarke, an elderly woman who often came with Mrs Nevin, arrived, crying about her friend, almost hysterical, demanding someone help her.

Julie, the receptionist on duty, tried to calm the woman, but Norrie would have none of it. She needed the doctor to come now, she said.

Jacinta finished with her patient, then took Norrie into the consulting room, but couldn't get much sense from her.

'Look,' she said at last, 'I've one more patient to see, then I'll come with you.'

She'd phone Mike once she'd sorted Norrie out. 'But in the meantime, you'll have to stop wailing and sit quietly. Would you like Julie to get you a cup of tea?'

Norrie's noise lessened, though not by much, and Jacinta took her back to the waiting room and waved the final patient in.

'Have you had a tetanus shot recently?' she asked the man, as she cleaned and bandaged a bad wound on his forefinger.

'Had one last week,' he said, holding up his other hand to show a grubby-looking bandage on it. 'I keep doing it. Shoving rubbish down in the paper-bin, although I know the night staff don't keep the paper and glass separate the way they should.'

He went on to explain his job as a cleaner in one of the pubs nearby.

'Next to that old building where the bag ladies hang out,' he added, as if to make the pub's position clearer.

'You mean Norrie—the woman who was out there. Is she one of the women?'

The young man nodded.

'Her and the old bat with the gammy leg. She whacks at me with her umbrella if I leave the rubbish bins over on what she considers "her" side of the back yard.'

He chuckled as if his battles with Mrs Nevin weren't all bad, then thanked Jacinta for her time and departed.

'Come on, Norrie, let's go.'

Jacinta grabbed her keys as she'd told Julie not to wait but to be sure to lock up as she left. She followed Norrie up the stairs and out past a couple of men in suits who were standing near the window of the adult bookshop with what looked like placards in their hands.

'This way,' Norrie told her. 'It's up this way.'

She led Jacinta up the mall, past the pub where the young man worked and into the entrance of the decrepit building she now remembered seeing, but hadn't previously taken much notice of.

'I can't get in,' Norrie complained loudly.

'You're not supposed to be able to get in,' Jacinta told her. 'Someone owns it, and they want to keep you out. It mightn't be safe to be in there.'

'But Bessie's in there, I know she is, and she must be hurt because she hasn't been out.'

'Is Bessie Mrs Nevin?' Jacinta asked, and Norrie nodded her ragged head.

Jacinta tried the door which, of course, was locked.

'Have you been around the back?' she asked Norrie, though she was by no means sure she wanted to get into the building. 'Can you get in that way?'

'Bessie says not to go that way. The publican don't like it.'

Or he might see them and report them to the police, Jacinta thought.

'Let's try,' she suggested, when lack of progress had prompted Norrie to start wailing again. 'We'll go down the side street. It's closer than going back through the clinic.'

Walking down the side street and into the lane reminded her of Mike. He'd be expecting her call but there wasn't anything she could do right now.

There was no obvious way into the building from the back, the entrance to what must once have been a coal cellar was padlocked shut and a fire escape ended some ten feet from the ground.

'Let's try the pub. Maybe someone there knows who has keys to the place,' she said to Norrie, and though Norrie cowered at the thought of entering forbidden territory, Jacinta had no qualms about knocking at the back door, then opening it and going in, calling as she went so no one thought she was about to rob the place.

Norrie, whimpering now, clung to her shirt, following so close she was treading on Jacinta's heels.

'What the hell?'

A man appeared, and Jacinta hurriedly explained.

'There's any number of old women hanging around the place, but I'm not their keeper and no one pays me to look after the place,' the man said.

'Do you know who owns the building?' Jacinta asked.

'Look, lady, I don't even know who owns this pub. I work here, that's all.'

He began to walk away, then apparently relented, turning back to say, 'The best bet is to phone the police. They can break in. Come this way—you can use the phone in here.'

Norrie, whose wailing had increased at the mention of the police, backed away, but it seemed like a sensible idea to Jacinta so she followed, feeling in her pocket for the scrap of paper with Mike's number on it. She'd phone him at the same time, explain she'd been unavoidably delayed.

She smiled to herself as she imagined his comment. 'More

lame ducks, Jacinta?' he'd probably say, but she'd hear his smile in his voice as he said it.

The police took some convincing that they should break into a building on the off chance a bag lady might be injured inside, but eventually Jacinta persuaded them to at least come and have a look.

The phone call to Mike wasn't much more successful. He sounded harassed himself, said he understood and asked if she'd phone when she was free.

He must have people in his office with him, she told herself, but disappointment that she hadn't heard the smile in his voice bit into her confidence.

Norrie was backed against the wall outside and nothing would convince her she needed to talk to the police.

'They won't listen to me because I don't know for certain Mrs Nevin sleeps here,' Jacinta threatened. 'They'll just walk away—do nothing!'

She must have sounded desperate because Norrie accompanied her back to the front entrance to the building, though she drew back into the shadows when two policemen arrived.

'The building's listed as belonging to a company, with a solicitor's office as the address for mail. No one there this morning, of course, and the only person we could get hold of from the solicitor's firm had never heard of the company.'

The older of the two policemen explained this to Jacinta as soon as they'd introduced themselves. Then he asked again who Jacinta was and how she'd come to be involved.

'The pub cleaner confirmed that a number of elderly women, including Mrs Nevin, use the building, which is why Norrie might be right. Mrs Nevin has a bad leg—she *could* have fallen and be lying injured in there.'

'Are you prepared to pay for any damage we do if it becomes an issue with the owners?' the policeman asked.

Jacinta frowned. She glanced at her watch. It was already after two and her time with Mike was dwindling rapidly. Now it seemed she was going to be up for the cost of a new door if she pushed the policemen into breaking this one down!

She glanced at Norrie, and saw entreaty in the faded old eyes.

'I'll pay for it,' she said, and stepped aside.

Breaking down a door was nothing like she'd imagined it would be. The younger policeman simply aimed his boot at the lower hinge, and when it gave way with a splintering of wood, the door sagged, releasing the lock.

'We'll have to board it up after,' the older man remarked to Jacinta. 'You'll pay for that as well?'

She nodded and followed the two men inside, smelling dust and damp, and something else.

Cooking smells?

Norrie had dashed away, scuttling like a crab up a curved staircase to disappear out of sight on an upper floor.

'Follow her,' the older policeman said to his colleague. 'You and I'll look around down here,' he added to Jacinta.

Signs of recent occupation were everywhere, but there was no sign of Mrs Nevin. Then the younger man called out.

'We'll need an ambulance. Can the doc come right away? She looks bad.'

Jacinta raced up the stairs, following the sound of Norrie's wailing. Mrs Nevin was unconscious, lying in a curiously twisted way beside a tipped-over metal chair.

Jacinta knelt beside her, feeling the faint flutter of a pulse below the woman's jaw. The younger policeman was despatched to call an ambulance and wait downstairs for its arrival.

'She was putting up the blanket,' Norrie whimpered, kneeling on the other side of the woman. 'She liked to live in different rooms but put the blanket up so the light didn't show.'

Jacinta was gathering up coats and blankets slung haphazardly around the room, wrapping them around the unconscious woman, while the policeman was going through Mrs Nevin's handbag, no doubt in search of identifying documents.

'Do you know if she has any relatives?' he asked Norrie.

Norrie shook her head.

'Just her that I know, though she lets a few of us sleep here. If we don't bring drink. She doesn't like the drinkers, but she forgot to open the door last night so I knew something must be wrong.'

'There's a bunch of keys here. They might be for the doors. Wonder where she got them.'

The ambulancemen arrived and started a saline drip then lifted Mrs Nevin's frail body onto a stretcher. The older policeman gave orders to the younger, telling him to get someone in to secure the building and to stay until it was done, while Norrie, apparently realising her chances of sleeping there that night were disappearing with Mrs Nevin, began to wail again.

'Come to the hospital with me,' Jacinta suggested. 'We can't just abandon Mrs Nevin, and as we don't know of any relatives, you can stay there with her.'

Norrie brightened perceptibly, then Jacinta remembered she had no transport. The suggestion they get a cab pleased Norrie even more.

So, instead of heading off for a weekend of sensual pleasure with her new lover, Jacinta found herself in the familiar confines of the A and E department, awaiting the results of Mrs Nevin's tests and keeping Norrie as calm as possible under the circumstances.

She phoned Mike, her voice pleading for his understanding as she finished her explanation.

'So, you see, until I know what's happening and can arrange something for Norrie, I can't really leave.'

'I do understand,' he said, and added, 'Phone me when you can get away. Maybe we can salvage something of the weekend.'

Jacinta felt a chill creep through her blood—where tingles had been earlier.

It's because he's been working and he's tired, she told herself. And he's disappointed.

She even began thinking it might be for the best. If Mike couldn't handle her chaotic working hours, then it was best they ended whatever they had now—before they both became more involved.

But her heart didn't believe it, beating erratically at the thought of not seeing him again.

By four, Mrs Nevin had been tested, assessed and admitted to a ward. Her hip was broken and a replacement operation had been scheduled for Monday. In the meantime, she'd be given fluids and antibiotics and kept as pain-free as possible. No relatives had been found, so Jacinta gave her address and various phone numbers as a contact for the woman.

All that was the easy part. Having co-operated as fully as possible, Jacinta now sought a little co-operation herself.

'Norrie is her friend,' she explained. 'Can she stay?'

The sister on duty surveyed Norrie doubtfully.

'While I'm on duty, but I can't guarantee anything later.'

The thought of the elderly woman being turned out at the end of visiting hours that evening, in a strange part of town and with nowhere to go, disturbed Jacinta, and she was fretting over it, wondering if she could ask her mother to collect Norrie later, when Mrs Nevin regained consciousness.

Far from wanting to know where she was or what she was doing there, all she wanted was her handbag.

Jacinta pulled it from the little cabinet by her bed and handed it to her, then watched the thin, frail fingers fumble in it, finally producing the keys.

'This is the key for the front door,' she said to Jacinta. 'You'll have to open it up each night about ten. Just unlock it but leave it closed, so the girls can come in. There's Norrie and Jess and sometimes Alison. No one else. The place isn't a dosshouse, you know.'

Jacinta closed her eyes and wondered if she'd strayed into a nightmare.

'They know they've got to be in by twelve and I lock it again then. I don't want hooligans or thugs bashing us up.'

Realising Mrs Nevin was too weak for an argument, or to be told the lock no longer worked, Jacinta took the keys, but had no idea what she was going to do with them. Or with

Norrie, Alison or Jess. Unless, of course, Mike could be persuaded that a night in an abandoned building on the edges of the city was a sexy alternative to whatever he'd planned.

She dropped the keys into her own handbag, found a ten-dollar note and gave it to Norrie.

'For something to eat and cab fare back to the city if the nursing staff won't let you stay,' she said. 'The cab fare is about five dollars, so keep that much.'

'And you'll let me in?' Norrie said, hope gleaming in her eyes and shaking in her voice.

'I'll do whatever I can,' Jacinta promised.

What she should do was walk away. She knew there were massive problems among homeless people, and had chosen to help the younger street dwellers, deliberately closing her eyes, mind and conscience to these older people so she could focus on the young.

Now she had keys to a building, probably illegally as there was no way Mrs Nevin had a right to them, but the door would be boarded up so keys were no good anyway.

All the way back to work, she worried about it, but when the cab dropped her in the back lane she was no closer to a solution.

Once back in the clinic she settled into the chair behind her desk and pulled out her file of charitable organisations that provided services for the needy. And started phoning them.

By the fifth call she was ready to despair when a man said, yes, he'd be willing to wait at the building from ten to twelve and take any women who turned up there back to his shelter for the night.

'We have dormitories for men and women, and I've a van to pick up strays. I'm usually on the street from midnight, so the two hours won't make much difference.'

Jacinta thanked him and was about to hang up when he said, 'Hey, not so fast. I know the mall and Abbott Road Clinic, but where's the old ladies' building? I can get away now, be there in about ten minutes. Could you meet me at the mall entrance to your clinic and show me where to go?'

Jacinta agreed, then listened to the man describe himself as overweight and balding.

She disconnected, and her fingers hesitated over the keypad of the phone. She should call Mike and tell him she'd be ready in half an hour, no later, though something in the way he'd sounded earlier made her reluctant to make the call.

But indecision was making her edgy, so she dialled and heard his voice—the deep, husky voice she knew.

'Poor mouse,' he murmured. 'What a torrid day you've had. Would you rather cry off the weekend? It's up to you. I can pick you up and take you straight home if you'd prefer that. Maybe do something with you tomorrow? Or we can go away as planned. How do you feel? Tell me what you want.'

Jacinta was overwhelmed by the emotion his gentle understanding generated in her body.

'You come, and we'll decide then,' she managed to say, though her voice was trembling as much as her body. 'I'm sorry it's been such a mess.'

'Don't apologise,' he told her. 'You've no idea the amount of work I've got through, trying to keep my mind off seeing you again.'

They arranged to meet in the car park at the back of the building, as Mike had returned his keys to the security people.

'I've missed you,' he whispered as they said goodbye, and Jacinta held the words to her as once again she locked her room, set the alarm and went up the stairs to the mall.

A huge man was standing there, peering down the stairs.

'Dr Ford?' he said. 'I'm Neville.'

'And I'm Jacinta,' she told him, shaking his hand then indicating which way they'd go.

'Sorry to make you do this, but it would be dreadful if I was waiting in the wrong entrance and missed the women,' he said, and Jacinta waved away his apology.

'I'm just so glad you agreed to help. I couldn't think what else to do. Even with keys, I was chary about the legalities of letting people into the building, though now the door's been boarded up the keys weren't much use.'

She led him past the pub and into the entrance of the building next to it.

The door's at the back here. It's one of those old three-storey places, and there's no lift. Just inside, the stairs wind up and up. It's a wonder none of them have been injured in it before.'

Neville had a good look around, and seemed content to linger for a chat, but Jacinta knew Mike would be waiting, and she'd already ruined half his day.

She excused herself, told Neville to feel free to look around and hurried back down the mall. If she'd thought to take her overnight bag with her, she could have gone down the side street and along the back lane, and saved herself the bother of locking and unlocking the doors, not to mention disarming and rearming the alarms.

But then she'd have missed the signs!

She stopped dead in front of the adult bookshop window and stared in disbelief. The 'placard' she'd seen earlier had been erected and the sign read FOR SALE BY TENDER, in letters so red they looked like blood. 'Inner city building, ideal re-development proposition' it went on, then mentioned land area, zoning possibilities and a real-estate agent who'd be happy to arrange a deal.

Mike was selling Abbott Road.

Mike, who was probably waiting in his fancy Jaguar, right now behind this building, was selling it, closing them down. He must have known because signs like this weren't made overnight.

And he hadn't told her.

CHAPTER ELEVEN

JACINTA'S anger built as she unlocked doors and fumbled with alarms, until finally she stormed into the back yard in time to see Mike's car glide to a halt.

He switched off the engine and opened the door, his delight at seeing Jacinta emerge from the building wiping away some of the frustration of the morning.

Then he noticed the scowl on her face, the pent-up fury in her eyes, and realised the virago had returned.

'You're selling the place and didn't think to tell me? You let me paint it, fix the chairs, talk about restructuring, and all the time you had no intention of keeping Abbott Road.'

He took hold of her shoulders, hoping to calm her, but small fists beat against his chest as she continued her tirade.

'It's all about money, isn't it? You can't even commit to a lasting relationship because you're so hung up over losing a few of your millions if it didn't work out. You're a pathetic excuse for a man, Mike Trent, and I'm glad I found out about it before I fell even more in love with you.'

And with that she tore herself out of his arms and raced back to the building, slamming the door and, no doubt, setting the alarms, before he'd taken two steps.

Mike stared at the closed door, and felt his own anger mounting. How dared she rave and rant at him when he'd spent the whole morning in a fruitless endeavour on her behalf?

She'd not even stayed to listen to his side of the story!

He'd tell her now—throw a few words at *her* for a change.

Though maybe it was for the best, he decided as his anger began to cool and rational thinking returned, that things had ended now, before they became too involved with each other.

But the ache in his chest gave the lie to the thought, and the rest of the weekend stretched before him like a vast desert of emptiness.

He leant against the bonnet of the car, folded his arms and closed his eyes. There was a way out of this somewhere—if only he could find it.

His mobile buzzed and he snatched it from his pocket, praying it was Jacinta, calm now, wanting to talk, but the voice, though familiar, wasn't the one he desperately wanted to hear.

'What's going on with Libby?' Lauren demanded. 'Is she using "something on at school" as an excuse to go to you tomorrow, instead of coming to me? And what are you letting her get away with that she'd want to go to you?'

Mike lifted the phone away from his ear and looked at it, though that didn't help him make sense of Lauren's words. Then he thought of a similar message he'd received himself, and frowned.

'Libby's not coming to me tomorrow and, in fact, she didn't come last time she was due to. I didn't speak to her but she phoned Dad with the same excuse—"something on at school". Do you think she's up to something?'

He doubted it even as he spoke—Libby had always been honest with him.

'She's almost a teenager, Mike,' Lauren said in a long-suffering tone. 'Teenagers are always up to something.'

Worry niggled in his gut. Between his daughter and Jacinta, he'd have an ulcer by Monday.

'Did you phone the school?'

Lauren laughed, but it was a harsh, discordant sound. 'And admit to those prissy women that I don't know what my daughter's doing? You chose the school, you phone it.'

Mike sighed.

'I'll call you back.'

He pressed the code for the school's number, introduced himself and asked if he could speak to the house mistress on duty. Worry that his daughter might not be happy at the school added to his growing burden of anxiety. When Lauren had insisted that Libby go to boarding school, leaving her and her new husband free to travel the world, Mike had objected, but his own living arrangements and work hours were such that having her live with him was impossible.

Though if he hired a full-time housekeeper...

Or married Jacinta?

'Mr Trent? Jillian Frost here.' A woman's voice brought him out of the realm of conjecture, though the final thought had been so mind-blowing Mike had felt his stomach knot. 'Did you want to speak to Libby? She won't be back from their sporting fixture until after seven. It's a two-hour bus trip.'

'No, I was wondering about tomorrow. Her mother tells me she's not going to her, and Libby cancelled her Sunday with me a fortnight ago, so we were worried there might be something upsetting her.'

'Tomorrow?' Miss Frost said vaguely, then something must have clicked into place. 'Oh, it's another onslaught out at Ellerslie House. It opens next weekend and I think tomorrow the plan is to help with the landscaping. "Kids Helping Kids", you know.'

The 'kids helping kids' phrase rang a vague bell, but the rest of the explanation might as well have been in Swahili for all the sense it made to Mike.

'No, I don't know,' he said bluntly. 'Somewhere along the line I've missed something.'

Miss Frost explained how the group had originally been set up as a community project within the school curriculum. 'Wednesday afternoons, in school time, when pupils do work in the community,' she reminded him. 'Libby's group somehow heard about this house being set up as a permanent home for street kids, and wanted to work there. Originally there was a lot of cleaning, then painting—things they could do to save the costs of having professionals in.'

Was it the house he'd heard about last Tuesday evening?

'Anyway, as the countdown to the official opening began, there was mass panic that it might not be finished in time, hence the Sundays given over to it as well.'

'If they need extra physical labour in the yard, I'd be happy to help,' he heard himself offer. 'Give me a chance to catch up with Libby as well. Do you have the address?'

Miss Frost was only too delighted to give it to him, assuring him that the more helpers they had, the better.

Which didn't mean Jacinta would be there, he told himself.

Jacinta arrived home to a deserted house. She knew her mother and Fizzy would be over at Ellerslie House. At least now she could cook them a hot meal to come home to, and be available herself to help tomorrow.

But no one came home to dinner, though preparing the meal had given her something to do apart from thinking about Mike and the shattered state of her heart. She packed the food into containers and dumped them in the refrigerator and left a note for her mother. 'I'm home, don't ask, wake me in time to go with you in the morning.'

And went to bed, though not to sleep.

Mike was a businessman—she'd known that all along—and selling Abbott Road was, no doubt, a sound business decision. So shouldn't she have listened to him this afternoon instead of ranting, raving, hitting him, then storming away?

I'd have listened to him if he'd told me instead of letting me find out like that, her head argued. If he'd been honest with me about it.

But being right, or even part-way right, didn't ease the tightness in her chest, the bruised feeling around her heart or the aching sense of loss that had invaded her body like an untreatable virus.

She heard her mother and Fizzy return, voices and footsteps, the sounds of bedtime and quiet goodnight calls. But instead of feeling comforted by their presence in the house, Jacinta's sense of loneliness intensified.

They were late arriving at Ellerslie House next morning, as her mother, apparently, had slept in. Jacinta suspected it had been done deliberately, but as they were all maintaining a polite façade and no one was asking awkward questions she didn't raise the subject.

'The ''Kids Helping Kids'' group from your old school are all here again,' her mother remarked, as they parked behind a big white van with a wheelchair lift at the back. 'It's wonderful how enthusiastic they are.'

Jacinta forced her mind away from the death of her relationship with Mike and agreed that the group, formed after she'd spoken at her old school, had indeed been helpful.

'And look, for heaven's sake, that's Ted Trent over there,' her mother added, pointing to where laughing schoolgirls were loading a man in an electric wheelchair with potted plants. 'He's being used as a self-propelled wheelbarrow by the look of things. I'll just pop over and say hello.'

Fizzy had already moved away, so Jacinta was deserted, looking towards the man in the wheelchair, wondering how badly disabled he was—and if he drove himself or if someone had driven him.

And what was he doing here? Had her mother asked him to come? Was there more to her mother's friendship with him than conversations about broccoli?

'That's all I need!' she muttered to herself. 'Mum to become involved with Mike's father!'

But the question of how Ted Trent had got there took priority over her mother's interests right now, and Jacinta glanced back towards the white van.

If the van with the ramp was his, then he probably didn't drive himself.

Though maybe he had a friend who drove him places. Or a chauffeur. Mike could afford it.

'Are you here to help or just to admire our industry?' Bonnie called to her.

With her heart beating so hesitantly she thought she might faint, Jacinta stepped slowly into the yard.

'The girls are doing the planting down the side fence,' Bonnie told her. 'The nursery donated not only all the plants but a chap to supervise where and how to plant them, so he's in charge there. He's young and gorgeous so the girls are falling over themselves to help.'

'I can see that,' Jacinta said, wondering why the girlish laughter should be jarring so badly on her nerves. 'What can I do?'

'Lay turf?' Bonnie asked. 'It's in big rolls. The boys are out the back, raking and levelling the soil, and as they do one patch we need someone to roll out the strips of turf. It's out there as well, a great pallet of it a lawn company donated. People are *so* good, aren't they?'

Bonnie was so pleased with the world Jacinta wanted to bite her, but she moved obediently down the drive on the far side of the house towards the back yard.

Rolling out turf sounded like the kind of hard physical work she needed. Something to exhaust her body so, hopefully, her mind would stop its ceaseless circling, around and around in ever-increasing whirls of misery.

But Mike was there, stripped to the waist like Will and Dean, shovelling sand from a heap into a real wheelbarrow, while the boys wheeled and tipped and raked it smooth.

'Hi, Jacinta.' Will greeted her with delight. 'Fizzy said you wouldn't make it. Something about going away. But I knew you wouldn't want to miss such an exciting job. Do you want to rake?'

She'd seen Mike turn when Will had called to her but, though he'd nodded briefly, the pile of sand was now demanding all his attention.

'No, I'm here to roll turf. Just tell me where to start.'

'I'll help you,' Dean offered. 'I'll carry the rolls and you can spread them out. Mike and Will can manage the sand.'

Jacinta's eyes strayed to where Mike was 'managing' the sand, and her fingers tingled as she remembered how those rippling muscles had felt beneath her hands.

She followed Dean to the pallet of turf, wondering about Mike's presence—and whether her mother had anything to do with it.

'I'll kill her!' she muttered to herself, startling Dean with her vehemence. But he didn't ask who'd prompted the murderous remark, simply lifted a roll off the pile and carried it to the back fence.

Jacinta lifted another one and followed him, surprised by the weight of grass and the thin layer of dirt beneath it. Following Dean's lead, she bent and unrolled it, then found a smile for him.

'You look at if you've done this before,' she said, and he responded with his own shy smile.

'I want to work in landscaping. We've done this in the Saturday morning course I've been doing at the college. Landscaped the house where the deaf students have their meetings.'

The simple pleasure in his voice lifted a little of the sadness from Jacinta's heart. How could she be so overwhelmed by the pain of love when this lad had overcome the death of his mother, abandonment by his mother's lover and then the rigours of life on the streets?

Ignoring his protests that he'd carry and she could spread, she followed him back to the stack and carried the next roll into position. Then the next, and the next.

Mike watched Jacinta work, saw the way her knees buckled at times, and finally he broke.

'You finish the sand,' he said to Will. 'There's not much.'

Then he strode across to where Jacinta was struggling with a bigger than usual roll of turf.

'They're too heavy for you,' he growled, snatching it out of her hands and scowling ferociously down into her dirt-streaked and heat-flushed face. 'Dean and I will carry—you unroll them.'

He saw the fire flash in her eyes and knew she wanted to snatch it right back, but couldn't—which only made her angrier.

'What are you doing here anyway?' she snapped at him, following him to where the next strip would be laid. 'Come to crow, have you? To rub salt into the wound?'

'I came because they needed help,' he told her, bending to set the roll in place, 'but you probably won't believe that any more than you'll believe I didn't tell you about selling Abbott Road because I wanted to have alternative accommodation for the clinic lined up first.'

She was standing over him, hands on hips, a very grubby virago with the wind taken out of her sails.

'Alternative accommodation?' she whispered. 'You're not closing the clinic?'

The hesitation in her whispered words weakened Mike's determination to pay her back for her fury of the previous day—and for spoiling the entire weekend with her leap to a false conclusion.

Suddenly he wanted to say it didn't matter—that they could forget about it and go on from here. Damn it all, he wanted to take her in his arms and hold her close and promise her the moon and stars and a few planets as well. But her eyes had narrowed suspiciously, and he suspected this wasn't quite the moment for a declaration.

Jacinta studied him, trying to assimilate what he'd said— and wondering if any apology would be sufficient to undo the damage she'd done.

But it wasn't *all* her fault, Jacinta told herself. And there was still the commitment thing.

Forget the apology. It was easier to stay at odds with Mike.

Better, too.

Far better.

'Did my mother phone you? Tell you I'd be here?' she demanded. 'Is that why you came?'

His answering frown suggested that hadn't been the case. He asked, 'Why would your mother phone me?' Which confirmed her guess.

'I just thought...' Disappointment that he hadn't come to see her shafted into her lungs, but if her mother hadn't phoned...

'Why *are* you here?'

Mike grinned as if he'd followed every nuance of her tortuous thoughts.

'Would you believe so I could spend some time with my daughter? Though I must admit, the idea that you might be part of the working party did cross my mind.'

The grin had started her thinking things she shouldn't think, but the mention of his daughter diverted her enough to say, 'Your daughter? Where on earth does your daughter come into this?'

'She's working here. In fact, I think it's time you met her. And my dad.'

He turned to Will and Dean.

'You guys keep at it, OK? I need Jacinta for a minute.' He slipped his arm around her shoulders, tucked her close against his body and whispered silkily into her ear, 'Actually, I need Jacinta for far longer than a minute, but we've things to work out first.'

He guided her towards the bevy of young girls working on the planting.

'Libby!'

Jacinta recovered sufficient brainpower to stop moving. She even managed to step away from him, but when she looked up into his grey-blue—today—eyes, what she saw there made her mouth go dry.

So the words, when they came, were hoarse.

'Libby? Our Libby from "Kids Helping Kids" is *your* Libby? But she's a boarder. Why?'

Mike smiled at her.

'Yes, she's my Libby and the "why" is something you and I might discuss some other time.'

By then Libby had joined them, and once again Mike slid his arm around Jacinta's shoulders.

'Jacinta tells me you two know each other,' he said to his daughter, who was looking from one to the other with utter astonishment.

'But you don't know Jacinta, Dad,' she finally said. 'I asked you ages ago if you knew any of the doctors from the Abbott Road Clinic and you said no.'

'I didn't know her then,' Mike answered, his grip on Jacinta tightening. 'But now I do, and just as soon as I've given her a little time to get to know me better I intend to marry her.'

'Marry Jacinta? Oh, Dad, that's wonderful!'

Libby threw herself forward and hugged them both with such delight that Jacinta felt it wasn't the moment to disabuse Mike's daughter of the marriage idea.

'I'll go and tell Grandad. He'll be pleased, too. He's been so afraid you'd end up a lonely old misogynist.'

She dashed off with the energy of youth, leaving Jacinta uncertain what to say next. She stepped away from Mike again and eyed him warily.

'Marriage? You told me you didn't intend marrying *anyone*. You gave me sensible reasons,' Jacinta reminded him. 'Then suddenly you're making marriage announcements to your daughter.'

He grinned at her again.

'I know—I should have asked you first, but I knew you'd say you didn't know me well enough, or that you didn't like me, or make some other pathetic excuse, so I thought I'd get it all out into the open, then one day, if we ever get some time to ourselves, I'd ask you properly.'

He paused and reached out to take both her hands.

'But you must know, Jacinta, that we belong together. What I feel is so strong it *can't* be one-sided.'

She was struggling to find words—to find breath as well— when Mike looked beyond her.

'Word travels fast,' he murmured. 'Here comes my dad and, if I'm not mistaken, your mother close behind him. So if I'm definitely and absolutely wrong about all this and you feel nothing for me at all, now's the time to say so.'

She looked at him and read the pain of uncertainty in his eyes.

'I'm not saying yes,' she warned him, and saw a smile stretch his lips and the doubt fade from his eyes.

'I haven't asked you yet,' he reminded her, then once again he put his arm around her and drew her close, turning her so he could introduce her to his father.

'We're not getting married,' Jacinta warned the two older people, when she'd made the appropriate responses to the introduction and properly introduced her mother to Mike. 'We hardly know each other.'

'Something I aim to rectify if I can get her away from her lame ducks for long enough,' Mike said, holding Jacinta with one arm but keeping hold of Mrs Ford's hand. 'Have you any advice as to how I might do that?'

Mrs Ford smiled at him, her eyes lighting up in just the way Jacinta's did.

'I found it was a case of if you can't beat her, join her. I see more of her at meetings and at work parties like this than I do at home.'

Mike released the older woman's hand, and nodded.

'I guess that means we should get back to laying turf,' he said, resting his hands on Jacinta's shoulders to turn her in the direction of the back yard.

He felt the quiver of reaction his touch had generated, and felt an answering tremor in his own body. Leaning forward, he rested his lips on the shiny hair above her ear and added, 'Fast! Once it's done I can spirit you away from here and tell you properly how I feel about you.'

Which would have worked if Jacinta hadn't remembered Mrs Nevin.

'So, you see, I really should go and see her.' She finished her explanation, her eyes pleading for Mike's understanding yet again. They were at the front gate of Ellerslie House. They'd cleaned off most of the dirt under the outside tap, their relatives were gone and Mike was insisting she decide where they'd go for dinner—once she'd had a shower and tidied up. 'Even before I have a shower, I should see her.'

'Mrs Nevin?' Mike repeated, frowning down at Jacinta as if totally at sea, though her explanation had been clear.

'The woman I had the police rescue from the old building up the road. Yesterday,' she added helpfully.

'A building in Abbott Road? Was it number one hundred and forty-six?'

He'd obviously gone mad, Jacinta decided. Too much sun!

'I've no idea what number the building is. That's not the point, Mike. Mrs Nevin is. I should go and see her in hospital before I do anything else, if only to reassure her about the operation.'

He was still frowning, though not quite as fiercely.

'And you say she had keys to the building?'

'She gave me the keys,' Jacinta said. 'But they don't work, the door's boarded up.'

'It *has* to be her,' Mike declared, then the frown was wiped away with a wide sunny smile. 'Come on, what are you waiting for? Let's go.'

He hustled Jacinta towards his car.

'To think I spent all morning yesterday trying to track her down, and you were ministering to her like a guardian angel.'

Guessing from the startled look Jacinta was giving him that she had no idea what he was talking about, he started the car, pulled out from the kerb and explained.

'I'll admit I was going to close the clinic when the building was sold, but once you'd convinced me it was needed, I started to think about relocating it. I heard there was a building not far from the Abbott Road clinic that might be available for rent, but the solicitors who manage the place were worse than useless so my solicitor did a title search and came up with the owner's name—Elizabeth Nevin. Unfortunately, on the title her address was care of the same solicitors, so yesterday I spent a futile morning on the phone, chasing down every Nevin in the phone book in the hope I might find Elizabeth and talk to her direct.'

'You mean my Mrs Nevin *owns* the building?'

'Well, she lives there. Do you know her first name?'

'Norrie calls her Bessie—that's Elizabeth, I guess. But if she owns the place, she must have money—why live there?'

Mike smiled.

'Who knows? No doubt she has a reason. Hopefully, it's not so strong she'll refuse to consider leasing it to us. With the rent we'd pay, she could afford to move into serviced accommodation and have her friends move in with her as well.'

'And with three floors, we might be able to do other things—sick child care, for one. And meeting places for groups like "Optional Extras".'

Jacinta could feel excitement bubbling inside her as she considered all that could be done.

When...

If...

She glanced at Mike as he turned into the hospital car park and pulled into a vacant space. He was smiling as if she'd said something funny.

'Perhaps we should get the operation conversation over with first,' Jacinta suggested, trying very hard to be sensible and practical, though, since the 'marrying Jacinta' announcement Mike had made earlier, sensible and practical had fled and she'd been left with fancies and fantasies.

'Whatever you think,' Mike whispered, leaning over to kiss her on the lips in a not very sensible or practical kind of way.

But with such sweet intensity Jacinta felt her bones melt.

Eventually they reached the ward where Mrs Nevin was awaiting her operation, to find Norrie visiting, with Neville and a younger man Jacinta thought might be a doctor.

'I'm Peter Nevin, Bessie's grandson.' He came forward, introduced himself, then guided Jacinta and Mike away from the bed so he could explain. 'Her solicitor had been trying to contact her for days, and when he couldn't he got on to me and I flew in this morning. I knew she'd been living in the old building in the city and went there first, to find it boarded up and a police card tacked to it. I gather you're the doctor who got her out.'

He thanked Jacinta for her help and explained that once the operation was over he'd be taking Bessie home with him. '

'But she's worried about her homeless friends, so if I can lease the building for her, maybe I can provide for them with the income from that.'

'Which is where I come in,' Mike said. 'I imagine I'm the reason the solicitors were looking for her.'

Jacinta left them talking and went back to Mrs Nevin.

'Peter says I have to have the operation,' she said, and Jacinta smiled, glad someone could talk sense to the older woman. 'He'll see Norrie's taken care of, too, and the other girls, but you're still my doctor so you'll come and visit me, won't you?'

Jacinta assured her she would, though doubt assailed her momentarily. Would Mike understand she had an ongoing commitment to her various projects?

'Yes,' he said, when she asked him the question later. 'Which doesn't mean I won't get angry or frustrated at times when you break a date to rush after one of your lame ducks, or when you spend time away from me on one of your pet projects, but that's who you are and part of why I love you. And it's also reminded me of why I became a doctor in the first place, something I'd lost sight of while the business grew and demanded more and more of my attention. You've achieved so much, but just think of what we can do together.'

Jacinta smiled at him, and repeated words he'd said to her only a fortnight earlier.

'We can't solve the problems of the whole world, you know. Well, not immediately!'

EPILOGUE

'I MUST say it's the strangest assortment of wedding guests I've ever seen,' Ted Trent remarked to Roslyn Ford as the two of them stood on the terrace and watched the visitors straggling up the drive to Mike's house.

Bessie Nevin, walking with the aid of a stick, had Norrie as her partner, and in honour of the occasion both were wearing all the clothes from their plastic bags, plus large multi-flowered hats. Will, Dean and Fizzy, on the other hand, were clad in their best black jeans—only small rips in the knees—and black T-shirts proclaiming their allegiance to some grizzly-looking band.

Libby and her closest friends from school, defying the coolness of winter, were in miniskirts and skimpy sequinned tops, while the various Trent Clinic personnel invited had apparently considered the wedding to be the top social event of the year and had dressed accordingly.

The bride, three months pregnant because she'd been too busy to do something about not getting pregnant, was, in defiance of tradition, in the groom's bedroom, negotiating leniency for Rohan who, thanks to the new computerised prescription checks, had been found to be over-prescribing and also dabbling in naltrexone implants.

'If you're making this a condition of our marriage,' Mike said, keeping his mind firmly on the matter under discussion no matter how delightful his mouse looked in the soft creamy dress she'd chosen, 'then we'd better call it off right now, because he's done the wrong thing and *should* be struck off the register.'

Jacinta looked up at him, her soft brown eyes innocently meeting his.

'As if I'd make it a condition of marriage,' she said, and he allowed himself a small smile as he repeated the 'as if' softly to himself.

'I'd just like to be sure that we find out why he did it. It seems to me it has to be for money, and in that case he could be on drugs himself and should be getting help. There's really no effective drug rehab programme specifically designed for medical staff—'

'No!' Mike said. 'It's way beyond our understanding or resources. Besides, right now I'd rather you were thinking of me, not some other man. Today is the day I make you mine for ever. Today is for us, for you and me, with no worries, no concerns and definitely no lame ducks. OK?'

Jacinta smiled at him while her heart, still badly affected by his presence, fluttered with excitement and tingles travelled to her toes. They'd already achieved so much together, she and Mike, with CPR teams now going into offices and other businesses for on-the-spot training for employees and the 'Optional Extras' programme sponsoring a second permanent accommodation house.

But this was different. This was marriage. A joining of her life to Mike's—for ever.

'What about you? No second thoughts?' she asked him, and though the love and commitment in his eyes were enough of an answer, she felt a surging rush of joy when he said the words.

'Not a one!'

'And we're going to make it? No fear of failure?'

'Not for an instant, my dearest darling.'

He bent and brushed an almost imperceptible kiss across her trembling lips.

She breathed in to regain the breath he'd stolen, and looked into his eyes.

'OK,' she whispered, knowing without the slightest doubt that Mike was the one and only love of her life. 'If you're sure, I guess there's nothing else to say.'

She grinned at him, then added, 'Let's do it!'

But her voice trembled because the look in Mike's eyes made her heart flutters even worse and the knowledge of his love for her threatened to overwhelm her.

Libby met them halfway down the stairs, her eyes alight with excitement, and said, 'Dad, you know the new Abbott Road building, Mrs Nevin's place, could we use the top floor for a kids' disco—for under eighteens? The "Kids Helping Kids" group could run it and—'

Jacinta put up her hands and said to Mike, 'Hey! This has absolutely nothing to do with me. In fact, I was thinking maybe one of the youth employment services could use it, but a youth disco?'

She beamed at Libby. 'That's a great idea. Let's just get this wedding out of the way then we'll—'

'Jacinta!'

Mike's growl of warning made her chuckle.

'Just kidding,' she told him. Then she turned to whisper to Libby, 'We'll talk about it tomorrow night when Mike and I get home.'

And though Mike's second growl told her he'd heard her words, she knew it wasn't an angry growl. In the past six months, he'd not only become increasingly interested in her activities but had brought new innovations and ideas to them. Working together to help others, she'd come to realise that beneath the businessman's exterior there beat a heart as soft as ice cream.

'I love you,' he whispered in Jacinta's ear as, with Libby now stepping decorously behind them, they walked towards the wide terrace to greet their guests and take their vows.

And though Jacinta echoed the words and smiled into his eyes, part of her mind had snagged on her earlier thought. Ice cream!

Perhaps she should put some ice cream in the cool-box they were taking away with them for their 'honeymoon' up at Mount Merion, where the frame and roof of the new week-ender would provide them with shelter overnight. If sharing chocolate-coated strawberries had led them to this wonderful day, who knew what a little ice cream might do?

'I hope you're thinking about me, not youth discos, with that wicked little smile on your face,' Mike murmured as, their arms entwined, they stepped through the door.

'You and ice cream,' Jacinta murmured. 'And our honeymoon.'

He chuckled, and she snuggled closer, secure in his love, and in her own investment in the future.

Modern Romance™
...seduction and
passion guaranteed

Tender Romance™
...love affairs that
last a lifetime

Sensual Romance™
...sassy, sexy and
seductive

Blaze
...sultry days and
steamy nights

Medical Romance™
...medical drama on
the pulse

Historical Romance™
...rich, vivid and
passionate

27 new titles every month.

*With all kinds of Romance for
every kind of mood...*

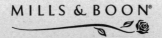

MILLS & BOON®

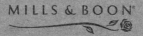

M253

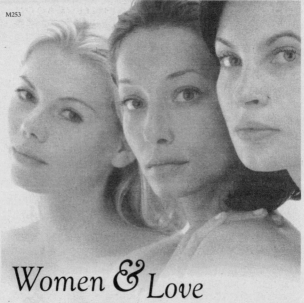

Women & Love

Three women...
looking for their perfect match

PENNY JORDAN

Published 19th July 2002

*Available at most branches of WH Smith,
Tesco, Martins, Borders, Eason, Sainsbury's
and most good paperback bookshops.*

MILLS & BOON®

heat *of the* night

LORI FOSTER
GINA WILKINS
VICKI LEWIS THOMPSON

3 SIZZLING SUMMER NOVELS IN ONE

On sale 17th May 2002

*Available at most branches of WH Smith,
Tesco, Martins, Borders, Eason, Sainsbury's
and most good paperback bookshops.*

2 FREE

books and a surprise gift!

We would like to take this opportunity to thank you for reading this Mills & Boon® book by offering you the chance to take TWO more specially selected titles from the Medical Romance™ series absolutely FREE! We're also making this offer to introduce you to the benefits of the Reader Service™—

- ★ FREE home delivery
- ★ FREE gifts and competitions
- ★ FREE monthly Newsletter
- ★ Exclusive Reader Service discount
- ★ Books available before they're in the shops

Accepting these FREE books and gift places you under no obligation to buy, you may cancel at any time, even after receiving your free shipment. Simply complete your details below and return the entire page to the address below. *You don't even need a stamp!*

YES! Please send me 2 free Medical Romance books and a surprise gift. I understand that unless you hear from me, I will receive 4 superb new titles every month for just £2.55 each, postage and packing free. I am under no obligation to purchase any books and may cancel my subscription at any time. The free books and gift will be mine to keep in any case.

M2ZEA

Ms/Mrs/Miss/Mr ....Initials......................................
                                                                    BLOCK CAPITALS PLEASE

Surname ....

Address ....

....

....Postcode................................

Send this whole page to:
UK: FREEPOST CN81, Croydon, CR9 3WZ
EIRE: PO Box 4546, Kilcock, County Kildare (stamp required)